Geri

A Post-Pandemic LGBTQ+
Novel About Something

Paul Lima

Geri

A Post-Pandemic LGBTQ+ Novel About Something

(Everything Seinfeld is not... but just as funny)

Paul Lima

Dedication: This book is dedicated to the Rainbow, including all my LGBTQ+ family members and friends.

Acknowledgments: I'd like to thank Richard Fisher for his excellent proofreading of the novel, and I would like to give a heartfelt thanks to Gabriele Pulpan for copy editing the book and making insightful comments that I took to heart when writing my final draft of *Geri*.

Note: I made a number of edits after the book was proofread. I did my best to avoid errors, but you may find the occasional typo. If you see a typo, email the error to paulmslima@gmail.com and I will correct the mistakes in the next edition of *Geri*. Of course, if you want to comment on the book, good, bad, or indifferent, email me.

"When all . . . are treated as equal, no matter who they are or whom they love, we are all more free." -- Barack Obama

"I hate the word homophobia. It's not a phobia. You're not scared. You're an asshole." -- Morgan Freeman

"I think being gay is a blessing, and it's something I am thankful for every single day." -- Anderson Cooper

"I've been embraced by a new community. That's what happens when you're finally honest about who you are; you find others like you." -- Chaz Bono

"We should indeed keep calm in the face of differences, and live our lives in a state of inclusion and wonder at the diversity of humanity." -- Jorge Takei

Author's note: Seinfeld has not formally approved this novel. Not that there is anything wrong with that.

Geri - First Edition 2020

Cover, interior design and content: Paul Lima. Copyright ©
2020

Published by Paul Lima Presents
www.paullima.com/books

ISBN: 978-1-927710-45-6

Contents

Chapter One

Geri Sender takes to the Klub de Komedy stage, with a red neon Klub de Komedy sign blazing behind them. They are mixed race, half indigenous and half white, in their early thirties, just over five feet tall, a solid build if somewhat slim-chested, wearing dark blue jeans, a tie-dyed pink t-shirt, and a carpentry belt with various tools in it. They pull up their carpentry belt which has slipped below their hips, brush back their rainbow-streaked black hair, place their hands to the sides of their deep-set eyes, and peer into the audience in the small, dark room. They take a deep breath and begin.

"We're four months into the year 2025. Two years after the coronavirus vaccine. Hope you've had your shot." They flex a bare arm. "I've had mine. Still red and kind of blotchy. But at least the headaches, nausea, and exhaustion have gone away. Not sure what's worse: the coronavirus or the reaction to the coronavirus vaccine.

"And we are officially five hundred years from 2525, the song by Zager and Evans recorded in 1968. They probably didn't think that man would still be alive or that woman would survive by 2525. Or they wouldn't have written such crappy lyrics."

There is no laughter. Not even a mild guffaw.

"Okay, you have to know the lyrics to get that joke. It's like the original computer coding guys didn't think there'd be a year 2000, hence Y2K..."

Again, no laughter.

"Anybody remember Y2K? No? Must be a millennial crowd tonight. Anybody want to sing 2525 with me?"

There is some nervous shuffling of chairs in the audience.

"Ah, that explains the zero hits for the song on YouTube." They clear their throat. "You know what song has a billion hits on the Tube? Breakin' Up Is Hard To Do. Speaking of which, my partner, ex-partner, found it easy to do. She says, 'If you get a penis, then I can't get with you.' Now I don't know for certain that I want a penis. I think I do. But balls? Those wrinkled, dangly bits of flesh? How do guys put up with them? If I go for a penis, I wonder if it comes with balls? Maybe balls are optional. In which case, I'll pass. Just a dick will do. Stick shift."

At last, laughter.

"My partner, ex-partner--have to get used to saying that--still lives in the same house that I live in. Yes, today's modern relationship. All the issues of living together. No sex..." They pause a beat to mild laughter. "Between the two of us, we can't afford the rent. That's why two friends are moving in. Between the four of us, we still won't be able to make the rent, but hey, when we get evicted, we'll have a built-in moving crew..."

Geri does five more minutes of comedy to a few laughs, pulls their hammer out of their tool belt, twirls it like a gun, and slips it back into the belt. They take an exaggerated bow to a smattering of applause, and exit stage right.

They go backstage where they meet Gaston, a white comedian loosening up his vocal cords. Geri notices some white powder on Gaston's shirt. "You might want to wipe off your shirt before you go on."

"Thanks," says Gaston as he wipes the powder off his shirt into one hand and inhales it through one nostril. "Hey, good set."

"It was crap," says Geri.

"They applauded you off the stage."

"I presume that they were happy to see me go. Besides, I hear next to nothing when I'm on stage. It's as if I'm in a comedic trance. A great silence descends upon me. When I'm done, I exit stage right like Snaglepuss. Or did he exit stage left?"

*   *   *

"It's less than two months until Pride," Geri says to Ellie as they brush back their rainbow-streaked hair which is shaved at the sides but longish at the front with several colourful streaks flopping over

2

their eyes. "I know we're not together, but do you want to go to the Pride Parade with me?" They are sitting beside Ellie on a dilapidated couch, with strips of duct tape holding its faded tartan upholstery together.

"I don't see why not," says Ellie Kim, a waifish ponytailed early thirty-something brunette with an aquiline nose, high cheekbones, and skin that is a yellowish-red tone. Her faded blue jeans are tight. Her olive-coloured top is loose. "Unless you're with somebody else by then. Or I am. Not that I'm looking. In fact, if you were to tell me you've given up thoughts of getting a penis, I'd tell you that I've given up thoughts of breaking up with you." Ellie is eating post-dinner popcorn. "I will always be fond of you, but... Penis? A girl has got to draw the line somewhere."

Geri leans forward and reaches for some popcorn. "Hey," says Ellie. "You said you didn't want any."

"I changed my mind. Besides, you can't eat a full bag. You're just going to toss the leftovers."

Ellie holds up the clear glass popcorn bowl to the living room light, a bare bulb overhead dangling on a dark, twisted wire, and squints as if measuring the quantity. "Okay, but no more than three or four handfuls."

"Other than a penis," says Geri as they fish a fistful of popcorn out of the bowl, "I'd still be me."

"Shouldn't 'me' be 'they'?"

"I'd still be they? Me? They? Me is a neutral pronoun so I think it works. But I'm not sure. The non-binary dictionary has yet to be written."

Ellie laughs and scoops popcorn out of the bowl. "You know I still love you. I just could not love, or even like, a penis."

"Ah, when did you become so narrow-minded?"

"You were lesbian when we met. You became non-binary shortly after we moved in together. And now you think you might be transgender. As for me? Gay. Gay. Gay. No pecker for me, thank you."

"I'm evolving," says Geri.

"Let me know when you grow legs and can walk on land." Ellie reaches for the remote. "Anything good on tonight?"

Geri

Ellie is dressed for work in a faded blue denim dress and black leather flats. She is sitting on the couch eating breakfast when Geri comes out of the spare bedroom they are now sleeping in, wearing a ratty robe, yawning, and scratching their butt.

"How romantic," Ellie says and she spoons another scoop of cereal out of her bowl. "I think even if you weren't thinking of growing a penis, we'd be breaking up."

"I've got nobody to get dolled up for, doll," Geri says as they pull a bowl out of a cupboard in the tiny kitchen, place it on the cracked laminated counter, and fill it with cereal. "Did you make coffee?"

"Pot on the stove, no?"

"Have you seen my tool belt? I told Nadir that I'd fix his garage door hinges. He said he'd cut fifty dollars off the rent, which is two weeks overdue." Geri pours a cup of coffee. "I've got no rent money. A few bucks, if I don't buy new socks or underwear."

"I have a few bucks coming from my part-time minimum wage job today, but I have to shop for some food on my way home, or we don't eat. Speaking of work, I have an early shift at Rainbow Theatre. Box office administrivia. Frankie, our new recruit, has the late shift covered."

"Just think, if I was a better comedian, we'd have money, and I wouldn't have to do carpentry and repair work."

"But you're not, so you do."

"Thanks for the support. I'd break up with you if you hadn't already broken up with me." Geri puts down their coffee, pours milk into their cereal, and then picks up their mug. They look into it as if inspecting it and then move to the old armchair across from the couch, placing their bowl of cereal on the ottoman that does not match the chair or couch. "How goes the playwriting?"

"Got to go to work," says Ellie as she gets up and dumps her bowl in the sink.

"That bad," Geri says. "Hey, don't forget, Jorge and Krystal should be here sometime today."

"Maybe between the four of us, we can sort out the rent?"

"Maybe." Geri swallows a mouthful of coffee and mutters to themself, "But somehow I doubt it."

*   *   *

Thirty-something Jorge Costa is driving a Rent-A-Wreck car along Bloor Street. Krystal Orbit, a transgender woman, also in her mid-thirties, is in the passenger seat beside him, fidgeting with a rainbow-coloured facemask covering her nose and mouth.

"Ossington," Jorge says. He is black, short, on the pudgy side with a shaved head to mask his premature balding, and a five o'clock shadow even though it's not yet noon. He's wearing faded jeans and a black t-shirt because he thinks it is slimming. "I'm sure they said Ossington, south of Bloor. But where does Ossington hit Bloor? We've been driving on Bloor forever." Jorge has pulled the front seat as far forward as he can and his nose is dangerously close to the windshield.

Krystal pulls down her mask. "It's west of Yonge Street." Krystal is tall and elegant, in an awkward manner. She is folded into the front seat like an accordion. Her red dress is coming off one shoulder and riding up her legs. She's wearing a brunette wig, which she keeps on adjusting, when not fussing with her mask.

"We live, lived, west of Yonge Street. We are west of Yonge Street. Would you take off that mask so we can pull over and ask somebody?"

Krystal holds both hands over her mask. "If we're asking somebody, the mask stays on!"

"Krystal," Jorge shouts. "The pandemic is over. We've all got vaccine shots."

"Not the anti-vaxxers," says Krystal. "And you don't know what they look like. Could be anybody."

"Well it's not me, so take off the mask when you are in the car with me. You're making me feel like I have the virus."

Krystal adjusts her wig and tugs the mask down over her chin.

"I've been wondering," Jorge says. "Since blondes have more fun, why did you get a brunette wig?" He unwraps a stick of chewing gum and shoves it into his mouth.

"It was on sale at The Dollar Store... Hey look," Krystal says, pointing back at a road sign as they drive through an intersection, "Ossington."

* * *

Jorge pulls into the driveway of 479 Ossington Avenue, a semi-detached, somewhat dilapidated-looking, red brick house on the east side of Ossington between Dewson and College streets. Geri and Ellie rent the first floor. "We are here," he says.

"The eagle has landed," Kramer replies.

"Let's unpack and then we can take the car back to Rent-A-Wreck."

Krystal fusses with her rainbow-coloured facemask, which is still wrapped over her chin. She pulls it up, then down again. "I have an even better idea," she says. "Let's unpack and then you can take the car back."

Jorge shakes his head. "Then you have to give me your share of the car rental fee and transit fare because I sure as hell am not walking back."

Krystal opens her door and gets out of the car. She's in heels and walking awkwardly. She opens the car's passenger side back door and starts pulling out plastic bags and a pillow. "Transit fare I can do. I'll have to owe you my half of the rental fee."

Jorge gets out of the car and shouts across the roof. "Great. I lose my job, we lose our place, we can't afford a cell phone between us, and I have to fork out the full cost of the car rental, which I don't have!"

"Or," says Krystal conspiratorially, "you could just drive the car back, leave it on the lot, and scoot. They don't know where you live."

Jorge opens the trunk and pulls out two green garbage bags and a pillow. "They have my license. I had to leave it in place of a credit card, which I also no longer have."

"But your license doesn't have our new address on it. Since you no longer have a car you don't need your license."

"Hmmm," says Jorge.

Jorge and Krystal, arms full of bags and other paraphernalia head toward the front door. Krystal is staggering in her heels.

"I had to give them a phone number," says Jorge.

"And?"

"I gave them Geri's."

"We tell Geri to deny knowing you when they call. Case closed." Krystal bumps into Jorge, stepping on his foot.

"Ouch!" Jorge starts hopping and drops some bags. "Do you have to wear those heels?"

"I'm getting used to them. After the operation, I'll be wearing them all the time. Even in my sleep!"

"You know," says Jorge, "women do wear flats."

"Not this lady!"

As they reach the front door, they almost collide with Nadir Knight, the landlord, his wife Deepa, both in their mid-forties, and their eleven-year-old son, Armaan.

"Hello," says Nadir. "May we help you?"

"Thanks, but no need," says Jorge. "Just moving in some stuff."

"Timing is everything," says Krystal. "We were just going to ring the bell to let Geri and Ellie know that we're here." Krystal puts down some bags and shuffles her mask, lifting it from her chin back over her mouth and nose. "Have you had your virus shots?"

Each Knight holds up and flexes an arm. Krystal and Jorge do likewise. Then Krystal nods and pulls down her mask.

Nadir and his family squeeze past Jorge, Krystal, and their stuff. "Are you having a party today?" Nadir asks.

"Moving in," says Krystal as she picks up her bags and trips over the step leading through the front door.

Nadir looks at his wife who shakes her head.

"Cool," says Armaan as he picks up a Pink Floyd CD that fell out of one of Krystal's bags. "Retro."

"I have more," says Krystal.

"How long will you be staying?" Deepa asks.

"Not long," says Jorge.

Krystal shuffles her bags so she can take the CD from Armaan. "Until Jorge finds a new job or I have my surgery and find work. Whichever comes first," she says.

"Surgery?" asks Deepa.

"I'm transitioning to heels on a more permanent basis. Surgery is the last step."

"So if you'll excuse us," says Jorge with a chuckle, "we'll lock up when we finish unpacking." He and Krystal carry their loads through the front door.

"If you let me borrow your Pink Floyd, I'll lend you my Led Zeppelin," Armaan shouts.

"You're on," Krystal shouts back.

"Maybe you should go to the back and speak to Geri before we go shopping," Deepa says to her husband.

"I was just thinking that," says Nadir.

* * *

Geri is unscrewing rusted hinges from the garage door when Nadir comes to the back of the house.

"How is it going with the door?" Nadir asks.

"Good. But the door doesn't quite fit the frame. I can trim it to reframe it and add some wood to the bottom for a better look and fit, and then paint it so you can't see the added wood. But then you might want to paint the entire garage..."

"Or tear it down and rebuild," says Nadir. "It was a chicken coop almost a century ago."

"Tear down. That's an option."

"Okay. Hinges, reframing, and paint the door. Sounds like a bigger job than we discussed, so one hundred dollars off the rent?"

"Sounds fair."

"Speaking of which..." Nadir pauses. Geri says nothing. "May's rent is two weeks overdue."

"Ellie gets paid today but has to buy groceries. She lost her insurance company job a while ago and is earning minimum wage part-time at Rainbow Theatre, the community theatre she works for." They turn a loose screw that does nothing but spin in place. "I have a paid gig at the end of the week."

"Comedy?"

"Carpentry. The comedy clubs in Toronto pay very little. The queer comedy clubs pay even less." Geri pauses. "All the comedy clubs in the city pay very little or don't pay at all, unless you are headlining."

"And your friends? The ones moving in unannounced?"

"Ah, they're here?" Geri pulls pliers out of their tool belt and tugs at the screw. "It's only temporary."

"Yes, until one finds a job or the other one has an operation of some sort."

"You talked to them."

At the front door as they were coming in," says Nadir. He pauses and clears his throat. "You know," he continues, changing the subject, "I am in charge of organizing the bank's head office Pride gala. It will be held the Saturday before the Pride Parade."

Geri pries the screw out and starts to unscrew the next one in the hinge. "You've done okay for yourself at Canada One Bank."

"I have a business degree from university back home, and was able to find decent work here once I took some human resources night school courses."

"Three screws should be in this hinge," says Geri distractedly.

"I saw you on YouTube, doing your comedy routine. It was funny, although there must have been a sound problem because I couldn't hear the audience's laughter."

"Yes, sound problems."

"We lost our Pride gala comedian. Left for New York a couple of days ago. Says he is booked solid on a U.S. tour and won't be coming back for Pride. If you could tone down your routine for the corporate crowd, we could use you at our gala. It pays enough to cover rent for May and June."

"You mean we wouldn't owe any rent until…"

"July first," Nadir says. "But you'd have to make your routine suitable for our corporate crowd."

"Give me some time to think on it," says Geri as they successfully remove the hinge.

9

"You have three days," Nadir says. "Then I go to the next person on my list."

"Just how many LGBTQ-plus comics do you know?"

Nadir shakes his head. "Two months' rent. But I need to know in three days."

*   *   *

Jorge and Ellie, back from work, are sitting in the living room, Ellie on the couch. Jorge is in one of two chairs across from the couch, feet on the ottoman. Krystal is walking circles around the room, rainbow-coloured facemask around her chin, trying to stay balanced on her heels. Geri, finished their work on the garage door, enters the room, toolbelt around their waist.

"Hey folks!" he calls to Jorge and Krystal. "Welcome to our abode."

"Good to see you," Krystal says.

"Thanks for putting us up," says Jorge.

"Not a problem, as long as you don't mind sleeping on the couch and the floor."

"Ellie was telling us that you are, um, sleeping in separate rooms," says Jorge.

"But still loving each other," Geri says as they sit on the couch beside Ellie and playfully put an arm around her. "So how's the pasta?"

"Boiling. Not yet al dente," Ellie says. "How are the hinges?"

"Repaired."

Jorge shoves a stick of chewing gum into his mouth. "Ellie is not your real name, is it?" he says. "Your real name is a Korean name that starts with E, like Eunji."

"Did you look that up on Google?" says Ellie. "My name is and always will be Ellie. My folks were born in Coquitlam, B.C. I moved here to attend theatre school at Ryerson. What about Jorge? That's not a black man's name."

"Oh, this is a good one," says Krystal who plops down on the other chair in the room.

Geri

"My father was Slavic, my mother was Jamaican," Jorge says. "When I was born they flipped a coin to see who got to name me."

"So your father won," says Ellie.

"Here it comes," Krystal says.

"Actually," says Jorge, "my mother won. She loved dad so much, she called me Jorge."

"See," says Krystal, rubbing her hands together.

"My father got to give me my middle name."

"Casmir?" says Ellie.

"Wait for it." Krystal as he leans forward.

"Jamal," says Jorge. "He loved her too."

"JJ!" says Ellie.

"What about you Geri?" asks Jorge.

"Nothing fancy. I'm as indigenous as they come, post-colonization of the new world."

"The accounts for your perpetual sun tan," says Jorge.

"Sun tan is not a race," says Geri. "Not that it matters what colour I am."

"But when it comes to gender?" asks Ellie.

"I'm checking on the pasta." Geri gets up and goes into the kitchen. "Hey, who wants a beer?"

"Beer," calls Ellie.

"Way more beer," says Krystal.

"Way, way more beer," sings Jorge.

*   *   *

The four friends are sitting on the living room couch and the two mismatched chairs, plates in their laps, eating spaghetti.

"Sorry there's no table in the kitchen," says Geri. "We normally use the ottoman as our table, but there's not room enough on it for four plates."

"Laps will do fine," says Jorge.

"Delicious," says Krystal as she slurps back pasta, mask around her chin.

"Considering what we had for breakfast and lunch," says Jorge.

"We didn't have breakfast or lunch," Krystal says.

11

"My point. But yes, it is delicious."

"Sauce straight out of a jar," says Ellie.

"And pasta straight out of boiling water," says Geri. "Sorry about the lack of parmesan."

"Do you know how expensive parmesan is?" asks Ellie.

"Not a problem," says Krystal, rolling a forkful of pasta and lifting it to her mouth.

"You made quite the impression on our landlord," says Geri.

"He was there, with wife and kid. We had to say something." Jorge slurps at his pasta.

"Anyway, here's our apartment rental deal," says Geri as they put their empty plate on the ottoman. Ellie gets up and heads for the kitchen. "There's no more pasta," Geri calls after her. She turns around, sits back down on the couch, and tosses her empty plate on top of Geri's plate.

"So, what's the rental situation?" asks Jorge.

"Ellie quit a job a while ago. She didn't like being an insurance company secretary," says Geri.

"Code for got fired, but glad to go." Ellie slumps into the couch.

"But she's now working for the Rainbow Theatre."

"Part-time. At minimum wage."

"I'm doing some stand-up..."

"Earning less than minimum," says Ellie.

"About the same as you make for writing your play, the one that you are not writing," says Geri. "I have a few carpentry gigs coming up. And..." Geri pauses and rubs their nose as Krystal gets up and starts to totter around the living room.

"Don't mind me," she says. "I'm listening. Just have to keep practicing in these things. I don't know how we women do it."

"And?" asks Jorge.

"Nadir has asked me to do a stand-up gig at Canada One's Pride gala. Pays two months' rent." Krystal bumps into the living room wall. "But I'd have to tone down my routine for his corporate crowd."

Krystal leans against the living room wall and sinks to the floor. "So, we're in. Rent free for two months."

"Yes!" says Jorge.

Geri

"Not so fast," says Ellie holding a hand to her head. "I think I know what's coming."

"I don't know if I can do it. I'm thinking about it, but don't know if I can sell my comedic soul to the bank."

"What's to think?" says Jorge. He gets up and goes over to Krystal. "You take out this, that, and the other thing." He puts out his hand and Krystal grabs hold. "Add whatever, whenever, wherever. And we're two months rent-free."

Geri looks over their shoulder at Jorge pulling Krystal up. "That's easy for you to say. You don't have to do it."

"Hey," says Jorge, "if I could do accounting for a couple of years, then you can tone down one routine."

"You hated accounting, and you no longer do it," says Geri.

"I didn't hate accounting. I hated the company I worked for and didn't get along with the people I worked with. If I had to go back to it, I could," says Jorge.

"Good," says Geri. "Because if I don't take this gig, you might have to."

"Take the gig," Jorge says. He and Krystal sit back down in their chairs. "Take the freakin' gig."

"Krystal," says Ellie, "Any modeling gigs lined up?"

Jorge snorts as Krystal straightens her dress and wig. "My new job doesn't pay," she says.

"You're a volunteer?" asks Ellie.

"Not really," says Krystal. "I am doing what I have to do, physically and psychologically, to transition to who I should be. Money doesn't come with that. Thank goodness for health care."

"And I'm looking for a new job and a new relationship..." says Jorge.

"Not necessarily in that order," says Krystal.

"So money is a tad tight right now for all of us. So take the gig," Says Jorge. "For all our sakes."

"I'm thinking on it," says Geri.

"In the meantime," says Jorge, "if I can help you with anything you've got going, let me know."

"What do you know about carpentry, or comedy?"

Geri

"I can hold nails while you hammer them. Or hold wood while you cut it," says Jorge.

"Well now, that would be funny. You holding my wood," Geri says.

Chapter Two

Geri takes to the Klub de Komedy stage. They pull up their carpentry belt which has slipped below their hips, brush back their rainbow-streaked hair, place their hands to the sides of their deep-set eyes, and peer into the audience. They take a deep breath and begin.

"I am a half-breed. Since I am one, I can say it. Just like a black person can use the N-word. Half indigenous. Half white. Although my half-white side is half British and half Scottish. And my quarter Scottish side is half Irish." Geri pauses. "But it gets even more complicated. Because on my indigenous side, I'm half Algonquin and half Ojibway. But my Algonquin quarter is half Mohawk. Put it all together and that makes me completely miscellaneous."

There is laughter.

"And we won't even begin to talk gender. But I guess we have. Born female. Currently non-binary. But thinking of getting me a penis, which is why my partner is no longer my partner. 'I don't drive stick shift,' she told me."

Again, there is laughter.

"Not to change the subject, but I am changing the subject," Geri says. "I know that you are not supposed to knock the competition, but... Have any of you heard of Robert Sorbian? The straight white male comedian who is doing LGBTQ jokes, people of color jokes, and women jokes. Not as insult comedy like in the 1970s and 1980s, but as supposedly funny yet respectful bits that he has no right doing because he is not freakin' LGBTQ, not a person of color, and not female.

"Some people don't know who they are, or who they are not. But fact is, you are somebody and you are not somebody. I know what I feel and feel that I'm not the me I was assigned at birth just because I had, or didn't have, certain bodily bits. I cannot feel who I am not. But not Robert Freakin' Sorbain. I mean I am not advocating putting a bullet in his head or anything like that. Maybe a sock in his mouth though.

"Speaking of not shooting people, I'd hate to be a cop today... Yeah, I know that I have to work on my transitions from one bit to the next." There is some laughter. "There are no good cops, that much I know. Even the nice guys and gals who are cops are not good cops. 'But I've never done anything nefarious,' they say. But you know cops who have. And you say nothing, do nothing. That makes you culpable. A not-so-good cop. A bad cop."

There is no laughter. In fact, there is almost less than silence.

"If you're not laughing. I don't blame you. It isn't funny."

Geri does five more minutes of comedy to some laughs, takes an exaggerated bow to modest applause, that in their comedy trance-like state they barely hear, and exits stage right.

Backstage they meet Gaston coming out of the washroom rubbing his nose. "Hey, good set," Gaston says.

"You can hear it in there?" asks Geri, pointing to the bathroom door.

"Well no, but I can hear them applauding you.

"They're just happy that I've left the stage."

*   *   *

Ellie, Jorge, and Krystal are weaving around each other in the small kitchen, pouring coffee, and taking out breakfast bowls and cutlery. Jorge is opening and closing cupboards. They are dressed to go out but have no place to be.

"No Cheerios? Only Raisin Bran?" Jorge says. "I hate raisins."

"I'll take them," says Krystal as she adjusts her wig and then tugs at the mask on her chin. "Pour your cereal and I'll take the raisins out of your bowl."

"That solves nothing. They've touched the bran. There is a residual raisin taste."

"I'd say 'have some toast,' only the toaster isn't working," says Ellie.

"Great. Bread for breakfast."

"For what you're contributing to the rent, be thankful for bread."

"And coffee," says Krystal. She lifts her mug as if to toast everybody.

Geri walks into the kitchen, wearing their ratty robe. "How was the couch?" they ask Jorge.

"Lumpy. My back is killing me. And there are no Cheerios."

"The floor?" Geri asks Krystal.

"Firm. Very firm. Maybe a bit too firm."

"I'm sorry we don't have a room and bed for you," Geri says as they pour a cup of coffee. "But since we're broken up we need separate rooms."

Krystal sits down on a chair with her bowl of cereal. "I'd be happy to sleep with you, in your bed," she says to Ellie.

"I won't sleep with them," she says nodding in Geri's direction, "because they're thinking of getting a penis. I'm not going to sleep with somebody who has one."

"But I'm getting it removed."

"Get back to me when it's gone and we'll talk."

Geri, shaking their head, sits on the couch with their bowl of cereal. Jorge sits on one of the chairs with his coffee and bread. "I'll shop for some Cheerios later. In the meantime, can I borrow your computer," he says to Geri. "I want to look for a job and, um, check the dating site I'm on."

"Not necessarily in that order," says Krystal, sitting on the other chair.

"You can borrow *my* computer," says Ellie as she sits on the couch.

Geri shrugs sheepishly. "Mine broke a while ago. Until we make some money, we only have one. I write out my routines on paper since we don't have a printer."

"And we can't afford Internet access," Ellie continues, "so I don't know what you'd do with my computer."

"How can you not have Internet access?" asks Jorge.

"The same way we don't have Cheerios, the toaster is broken and we can't pay the rent," says Geri. "You don't have a computer or Internet access either."

"Or a cell phone," chimes in Krystal.

Geri

"Something else we can't afford," says Geri.

"But we get by," says Ellie. "Besides, there's a library down the street across from the grocery store at College and Ossington. You can log onto the Net there. It's what I do. You just can't access porn."

"Doesn't your landlord have Wi-Fi? Can't you log on using his account?" asks Krystal as she plunges a spoonful of Raisin Bran into her mouth.

"Yes, he does. He shares it with us, but he changes the password when the rent is overdue," says Geri.

"I thought you were going to pay the rent by doing a comedy routine for the bank's Pride gala," Jorge says.

"I'm still thinking about it. I have to get back to him soon," says Geri. Then they change the subject. "You know that comedian I've talked about, Gaston."

"Sure," says Ellie. "I forget... Is he any good?"

"The thing is, he is. But I don't think he knows it. He is stoned on stage. Cocaine. He snorts in the bathroom before he goes on."

"I thought that was a comedy cliché," says Ellie.

"Not anything I've had the desire to try. Hell, I only smoked grass a couple of times. It made me paranoid. No fun at all."

"Ah, that's one thing I've always liked about you. Your drug-free sobriety."

"Yours too."

"And there's always beer," says Ellie.

"At least we can afford beer, once in a while," says Geri.

"More beer," says Krystal.

"Way, way more beer," sings Jorge.

Geri and Ellie laugh.

*　　*　　*

Jorge is in the library at a computer clicking through pictures of men, an open box of Cheerios on the table beside him. He clicks on a new picture, reads the bio beneath it, and reaches into the box for a handful of Cheerios, which he tosses into his mouth.

Geri

"Why not?" he says to nobody. "You'll do." He raises both hands above the keyboard, wiggles his fingers, and begins to type.

*　　*　　*

Geri and Krystal are sitting on the couch deeply engaged in a conversation.

"Have you really given up on modelling?" Geri asks.

"I don't know. I can't seem to focus on anything other than the operation. And even if a modeling gig came my way, I couldn't do it as the man I was, and I don't know if anybody would want to shoot me as the lady I am."

"Speaking of being a lady, how do you know you're transsexual?" asks Geri. "How do you know?"

"Oh, you know. You know," Krystal says.

"But I don't know, not for sure."

"Then," says Krystal with a matter-of-fact shrug, "you need to find out."

*　　*　　*

Ellie is in her bedroom sitting on her bed, covers in a tangled mess. Her laptop is open on her lap. She is moving her fingers above her keyboard, thinking but not typing. On the wicker night table beside the bed is a picture of her and Geri embracing. She looks at the picture for a moment, looks up as if sensing a light bulb above her head, leans forward, and begins to type furiously.

*　　*　　*

Jorge is walking by a clothing store for men. He unwraps a stick of gum, then spots a help wanted sign in the store window. He looks at the sign, then through the window of the store, and wraps his gum back up. He scratches his head and enters the store. A few moments later, a hand reaches into the store window and removes the help wanted sign.

19

Geri

*　　*　　*

Geri knocks on the door to the upstairs flat. They hear footsteps coming down the stairs. Armaan opens the door. He is eating an apple. "Hey man, how's it going?" he smiles and asks Geri.

"Hey," says Geri. "Is your dad home from work yet?"

Armaan takes a bite of his apple and shakes his head. He chews and speaks. "Not yet. My mom is home though."

"May I see her?" asks Geri.

Armaan calls up the stairs. "Mom! Geri needs to see you."

Deepa descends the steps. "Hello, Geri. What can I do for you?"

"How goes the volunteer work?"

"There are a lot of people like me who have had to flee their homeland. I can't solve their issues, but I try to help them adjust to their new home."

"Make it home sweet home for them?"

"Not quite. But not as bitter as it might otherwise be. Since I can't practice law in Canada, I do what I can, having gone through the process myself, to help new arrivals. Speaking of which, how may I help you?"

"Two things, if you don't mind," they say. "Can you tell Nadir I need to talk to him? And can we borrow your Wi-Fi password? I'm sure after I talk to Nadir he'd be happy to lend it to us."

"You are paying the rent?" Deepa asks.

"Sort of," says Geri. "Nadir knows how we are paying it."

*　　*　　*

Geri comes into the living room where Ellie is sitting on the couch, portable computer on her lap. She is typing but looks up when Geri enters the room. "Go ahead, ask," she says, all excited.

"Ask what?" Geri takes a seat on one of the chairs opposite her and puts their feet up on the ottoman. "I wanted to ask you if you were working the box office tonight."

"I'm home tonight. I work weekends with Frankie. Then we alternate weekday evenings."

"Frankie, eh? How's it going with the new recruit?"

"Going fine."

"And, how goes your play? That's what you wanted me to ask, isn't it?"

"It goes. It freakin' goes."

"And now for the big news of the night... Open the Internet connection. I have a password for you."

"No!"

"Yes. Wi-Fi. Enter, all caps, S-W-B-4-C-P-3-0."

Ellie enters the password. "Connecting... Connected! We have take off."

Krystal enters the room wearing a towel wrapped around her torso and one around her head. "Mind if I use your room to change?" she asks Geri. "It's that or the kitchen."

"Or the room you were in," says Geri.

"Way too hot and steamy in there."

"You've been in there for some time. We had to pee out back in the bushes," says Ellie.

"I'll be heading down to the Village, to Woody's. One always needs a good soak before heading down to the Village."

"Hell, I barely shower," says Geri. They wave toward their room. "Don't move any of the papers on my dresser. It's my next act coming together. Even the dust on the paper is important."

Krystal picks up a plastic bag at the end of the couch and heads to Geri's room. Jorge comes out of the room rather dapper-looking. Slim-fit jeans, a classic black dress shirt with a short button-down collar.

"At least Krystal has the decency to ask," Geri says.

Jorge shrugs. "You weren't in there."

"My, don't we look smart," says Ellie.

"Perks of the new job at Frederick's for Men."

"Well, congratulations. How much beyond your first paycheque will you owe them on payday?" asks Geri.

Ellie sniffs the air. "Cologne?"

"I'm heading out. With Thomas. And if I'm not back later, don't wait up!"

Geri waves the air in front of their face. "And if you are back, wash the stench off before you hit the couch."

"Too much?" says Jorge.

"Not at all." Ellie fakes a cough.

"Ah, what do you guys know," Jorge says. "I went back to the library after work. Had three replies to my profile. I'm meeting number one, Thomas, for coffee tonight. Number two, Mark, looks interesting. Not sure about Ramon, number three. He seems kind of hesitant and shy."

"A wallflower. Your type, no?" says Geri. "Oh, and I got a call from the car rental company. Denied knowing you, as requested."

"Many thanks," Jorge nods.

"See," says Krystal who has come back out of Geri's room. "Problem solved."

"Hope not to see you later tonight," says Jorge as he heads out the door. Geri and Ellie hear him in the foyer. "Go on in. They're not doing anything. You won't disturb them... Geri," he calls, "Nadir is here to see you."

Nadir comes into the living room. "Deepa said you wanted to see me. And that you asked for the Wi-Fi password, which I can change at any time."

"Should I give you two some space?" Ellie asks. "I should check my Facebook account sooner rather than later." She gets up and takes her laptop into her bedroom.

"I'm going into the kitchen to make some tea," says Krystal.

Geri motions to the other chair in the living room. Nadir nods and sits.

"I'll do it," Geri says.

"Ah," says Nadir. "For two months' rent and Wi-Fi."

Geri chews their bottom lip. "For two months' rent and Wi-Fi."

"And you will tone down your act, yes, for our corporate bank crowd?"

"And I will compromise my art for the sake of your corporate crowd

"Happy Pride," says Nadir.

"So freakin' proud," mumbles Geri.

Geri

*   *   *

The living room phone rings. Geri, on the couch watching TV, looks at their watch and wonders who could be calling at almost midnight. Geri answers the phone with a hesitant "Hello?"

"Hello. Is this Geri Sender?" an unfamiliar voice asks.

"Yes."

"This is Constable Phillips, Jason Phillips. From the Metropolitan Toronto Police."

"Yes?" Geri squints in a confused manner.

"Do you know a Krystal Orbit?"

"I do... Is she okay? Is she in jail?"

"So he is a she. That's what I thought. She is fine. A black eye, nothing more. He... She... got mugged by three boys when leaving the Village. She'd like to know if you can pick her up and escort her home."

"For sure. Give me your precinct address. I'll call a cab. Should be there within the hour."

"You don't have a car?" Jason says.

"I barely have cab fare," says Geri with a laugh.

"Tell you what. My shift is ending in ten minutes. Why don't you give me your address and I'll drive Krystal to you."

"Are you sure? You would do that?"

"Not a problem. I've been enjoying my interview time with her."

*   *   *

The door to the flat opens and Krystal enters with Jason, a tall lanky black man in uniform, behind her. "I hope you don't mind," she says, "but I invited Jason in for a late-night coffee."

"Mind? Not at all," says Geri. "More importantly, are you okay? What happened? Let me see that shiner. Where's your mask?"

"All will be explained," says Krystal. She turns to Jason. "Come in, come in, and thanks so much for driving me home."

"To serve and protect and all that," Jason says with a toothy smile.

23

"Have a seat," Geri says. "I'll put the coffee on. And Krystal, tell me what the heck happened."

Jason sits in a chair and Krystal sits on the couch. "It really was nothing," she says. "I left Woody's and was taking a shortcut to the subway stop on Wellesley, walking down a laneway, when three kids jumped out of nowhere, started calling me faggot, and took me down. But I got in some licks too. See." She holds up the bruised knuckles of her right hand to show Geri who is bringing cups of coffee into the living room. "They ripped off my mask, but my wig stood tall."

"Your wig was a tad dishevelled when we brought you in," Jason says with a smile.

"A tad, maybe, but still on my head."

"I hope you gave her hell for taking the laneway," Geri says to Jason while giving him his cup of coffee.

"Trust me," Jason says, "I did. But I don't know if it sunk in."

"I got a good look at them," says Krystal. "There was one of those motion detector lights on the garage I was passing when they jumped me. The light came on and there they were, three evil faces."

"She gave us a good description. They were probably kids from the suburbs. Regardless, chances of finding them are slim. But we know what they look like, thanks to Krystal."

Geri sits on the couch. "What a night. For you, not me."

"Krystal tells me that you are a comedian," says Jason. He sips his coffee. "One with problems with the police. She wondered about inviting me in."

"Hey," says Geri, "you've taken great care of Krystal, drove her home, and saved me taxi fare. I may have some issues with cops but trust me, all that you did is appreciated." Geri sips their coffee and puts their mug down on the wicker end table next to the couch. "You seem like a nice guy and you've been so freaking helpful tonight..."

"But?"

"Do we want to go there?" asks Krystal.

Geri

"I don't mind," says Jason. "I've only been on the force for two years, and the more I know about what people think, and why, the better cop I'll be."

"Okay," says Geri. "As nice a person as you are, and no matter how good at your job you are, you can't help but be a bad cop because there are no good cops."

"Interesting statement," says Jason as Krystal slumps. "Do tell me where you're coming from."

"Well," says Geri leaning forward, "I've had my run-ins with cops at protests and just walking on the streets. For instance, one time I witnessed an extremely rough takedown of a black kid by a cop so I started to film it on my cell phone, that was when I had a cell phone. All of a sudden, a second cop takes me down and smashes my phone. I was charged with obstruction. All I did was film an arrest. My case didn't go to court because the charges were dropped. It was like the charges were a warning shot fired across my bow: back off or else..."

"Sorry you had such a negative experience," says Jason. "As police, we often react when we don't know what's going to happen, to protect the public and ourselves."

"The public was being beaten by a cop."

"There are some over-aggressive cops, even bad apples."

"And some not-so-bad apples," says Krystal.

"It's not just that," says Geri. "I don't know how far you want to go with this."

"We're just talking," says Jason. "I promise my gun will stay holstered."

"Let me ask you this, then. Do you know cops on the take?"

"If I don't have to name names, I'll say 'yes'."

"Do you report them?"

"Well, no..."

"Do you know cops who have assaulted or wrongfully arrested black people, members of the LGBTQ community, or marginalized folks?"

"It happens, but it's nothing that I've ever done."

"Have you reported any cops who are on the take or have wrongfully arrested people?"

25

"No, but..."

"Are there other cops who don't commit such crimes?"

"A vast majority of us. Vast."

"But they know of such crimes, and say nothing?"

"Yes, but..."

"If I knew Krystal had robbed a bank..."

"Which I have not done and am not going to do," interjects Krystal.

"...and I said nothing, would I be breaking the law?"

"Depending on the circumstances, you could be charged with aiding and abetting."

"It's not my job to serve and protect, but I'd be breaking the law. But it's your job to serve and protect and you are not reporting crimes."

"It's complicated."

"Of course it is. You have a good job and you don't want to be ostracized by fellow officers or your union, so you say nothing." Geri reaches for their coffee which has gone cold and takes a sip. "Don't get me wrong," they continue, "I am sure that a minority of cops commit heinous crimes. But some do commit them. But no cops report the crimes, which is committing a criminal act. Hence all cops, even nice guys like you, are bad cops."

"He makes a point," interjects Krystal.

Jason rubs his forehead. "I know what you are saying, I really do. Growing up black, I had problems with the police and thought that by becoming a cop I could work to help change things from within. But it's not easy. It takes time."

"Trust me," Geri says. "I don't expect you to start reporting the bad stuff you know or to give up your job just because I have a beef with the police."

"Appreciate that," Jason laughs. "But I will think more about what you've said and the complexities of it all."

The three folks sit quietly for a moment.

"On that note," Jason says, breaking the silence, "I should take my leave." He gets up. "Krystal, do take care of yourself. Geri, it was good to meet you."

Geri gets up and they and Jason shake hands.

Geri

Krystal says, "I know the chances of you catching my assailants are slim, but if you do find them, I'd love to talk with them. Let them know that if they agree to meet with me, I won't lay charges."

"I'd want to throw the book at the assholes," Jason says. "But I guess that's just me."

"I'd join you in throwing the book at them too, I confess," says Geri.

Jason laughs.

"I'll walk you out," says Krystal.

When she returns to the room Geri is putting the coffee mugs in the kitchen sink.

"Leave them," says Krystal. "I'll wash up."

"Tomorrow," says Geri.

"Hey," says Krystal, "thanks."

"For what?" asks Geri.

"I've seen you talk about cops before with real hate and anger. You were almost gentle tonight."

"He is a nice guy. He really is. And he did bring you home."

"Not the point," says Krystal. "What I'm saying is that you pulled your punches. You didn't have to, but you did… You're worried that you can't pull your punches for Nadir. But you just did, so you can. Rent money here we come!"

Geri puts their head in their hands. "Oh my. I can compromise. Oh my."

Chapter Three

Geri takes to the Klub de Komedy stage. They pull up their carpentry belt which has slipped below their hips, brush back their rainbow-streaked hair, place their hands to the sides of their deep-set eyes, and peer into the audience. They take a deep breath and begin.

"So, Robert Sorbain's mouth is still sock free. The straight white male comedian is working vanilla clubs in the suburbs, getting paid to talk about the LGBTQ-plus community, people of colour, and women. All in an allegedly respectful, allegedly humorous manner. I don't know what's worse. What he says based on no personal experience or that he gets paid to say it." Geri runs a hand over their face as if to erase Sorbain from their thoughts.

"But I'd rather talk about a friend of mine, pre-op transsexual. She got mugged the other day. To demonstrate how ignorant they were, the muggers called her a faggot. Goes to show what they don't know.

"The cops think the muggers were kids from the suburbs. I don't know about the suburbs. Cookie-cutter families, with cookie-cutter kids, on cookie-cutter cul-de-sacs, in cookie-cutter houses... Okay, I have to stop saying 'cookie' because I'm making myself hungry.

"If the cops catch them..."--Geri pulls their hammer out of their tool belt, twirls it like a gun, and slips it back into the belt--"those kids are going to be in hot water. Speaking of which, we ran out of hot water today. That's why my hair is greasy. Didn't want to take a cold shower. Normally, it's greasy because I don't want to take a hot shower. Different tonight..."

Geri does ten more minutes of comedy to a fair bit of laughter. They end with, "Cookie. I gotta go eat." They take an exaggerated bow to a solid round of applause that they all but don't hear, and exit stage right.

Geri

*   *   *

Over breakfast, as all four friends eat cereal and drink coffee, Ellie says to Krystal, "What happened to your eye?"

"It ran into a fist last night."

"But you're a lover, not a fighter."

"Tell that to the three kids who jumped me."

"He's okay. A nice guy, at least for a cop, brought her home," says Geri. "And yada-yada-yada..."

"Yada?" says Jorge.

"Yada... as in he's okay and the cop and I had a long talk about policing and yada...."

"And the cop didn't shoot you?" Jorge asks.

"Geri pulled their punches," says Krystal. "They were rather magnificent. And the cop was a nice guy."

"For a cop," says Geri.

The friends eat cereal and sip coffee in silence for a bit, and then Ellie says, more to the room than to anybody in particular, "Guess who going out on a date tonight?"

"On Monday night," says Jorge as he chews a mouthful of Cheerios. "Who goes out on a date on a Monday night?"

"A person who works weekends and opposite weekday evenings as her date does, that's who."

Geri picks up their coffee mug. "So you're dating Frankie."

"I'm chaste until my transition is complete," says Krystal.

"I didn't say 'guess who is having sex tonight,'" says Ellie.

"So," says Geri looking at Jorge. "How was your date last night?"

Jorge takes a mouthful of coffee. Swallows hard. "Don't ask," he says.

"Okay, I'll ask," says Ellie.

"I was asleep when you got in," says Krystal.

"Snoring like a log," says Jorge.

"The date," says Geri before spooning in another round of Raisin Bran.

"Shitty. Worse than shitty," says Jorge. He puts his bowl of Cheerios on the ottoman beside his coffee mug. "We decided to go

29

for something light. Dessert and coffee. That way we could chat..."
His voice drifts off.

"And?" Ellie prompts.

"When the bill comes, Thomas, if that was his real name, looks at me. So I pick it up. Now he ate a more expensive dessert than I did, but feeling generous I say, 'Happy to go halves.' He looks at me like I'm nuts."

"But you are," says Ellie.

"So," says Geri. "Reconstruct the date for us."

"Okay," says Jorge, "but only from the bill."

Jorge: Happy to go halves.

Thomas: What?

Jorge: Halves. You had the more expensive dessert, but I'm happy to go halves.

Thomas: But you asked me out.

Jorge: No, I replied to your profile post, which the dating site said was compatible with my profile post.

Thomas: Which was you asking me out on a date.

Jorge: Kind of, but not really.

Thomas: Really, not kind of. And the bill, she is all yours.

"I won't go into the other weird aspects of the night, but..."
Jorge pauses dramatically. "I was out with a wing nut."

"You got back late, though, if I was asleep," says Krystal.

"Because when Thomas left, without paying a cent, I went to the midnight madness show at the Revue. Rocky Horror Picture Show. I got soaked and covered with toast."

Geri toasts Jorge with their mug. "Ah, to life on the wild side!"

"There were two more profile matches on the dating site. Before work, I'm going to the library to check them out."

"Or," says Ellie, "now that we have Wi-Fi, you can use my computer tonight while I'm on my... date."

*   *   *

Geri

Ellie burst out of the bathroom, a bath towel around her body and a smaller one around her hair. "There's no friggin' hot water."

Geri says, "I had a shower."

Krystal says, "And I had a soak after he showered."

Jorge says, "Don't look at me. I'm just a little piggy tonight."

Ellie sighs deeply. "Geri, since you will be performing to pay the rent, can you ask Nadir if there is anything he can do about this."

"I told him I was going to perform, but I'm not one hundred percent sure that I can do it."

"Well, while he thinks you are going to do it, can you ask him about maybe getting a larger hot water tank?"

"Or we could all try to use less hot water," Geri says, looking at Krystal.

*　　*　　*

Geri is in the front hallway, knocking on the door to the second floor. Armaan answers it. "You want to speak to dad, I guess."

"If he's in and not busy."

"I'll get him," Armaan says, and calls up the stairs.

A moment later, Nadir descends the staircase and Armaan goes back up. "Ah, Geri, so what can I do for you?"

"We ran out of hot water again tonight. Seems like it's going to be a regular issue."

"But the four-person living arrangement is just temporary, no?" Nadir says.

"It might be longer than first thought," Geri admits.

"Okay, then I propose a plan. Once you play the gig, I will look into the purchase of a larger hot water tank for you."

"So we've got two months of running out of hot water?"

"Perhaps set a shower schedule."

"You're not doing this as a way to ensure I do the gig?"

"You're not thinking of backing out?"

"No, at least not every day." With that, Geri returns to their apartment

"Well," says Ellie as she pulls back her hair into a ponytail.

"I have to do the gig, and then he'll look into it."

Geri

*   *   *

Geri, Jorge, and Krystal are sitting on the couch watching TV when Ellie comes home from her date.

"Kind of early," says Jorge.

"No Frankie in tow," says Krystal.

Geri hits the remote, turning off the TV. "Spill the beans. How was it? Who calls whom next?"

Ellie flops in a chair across from the three amigos. "Do you want me to reconstruct the evening for you? How about I just do the last bit, as it all comes crashing down?"

"I'm always up for a good story," says Krystal.

"Do tell," says Jorge.

"Not if it's too painful," Geri says with a grin.

Ellie sighs deeply. "The last few minutes." She reconstructs the end of her date.

Ellie: This has been fun. Would you like to come back to my place for a coffee?

Frankie: Didn't we just have a coffee?

Ellie: Okay, I'll air-quote it. 'A coffee.'

Frankie: Why did you just put air quotes around coffee?

Ellie: Are you going to make me say it? Okay, I'll say it. Do you want to come back to my place for sex?

Frankie: But I'm married.

Ellie. I'm sorry... I had no idea. What's her name?

Frankie: His name is Jack.

Ellie: Jack? As in you're straight, Jack?

Frankie: What did you think?

Ellie: But you work at an LGBTQ-plus theatre.

Frankie: Jack and I are working on having a baby. Since I had box office experience, I took this part-time gig until I get pregnant. During the interview, nobody asked if I was gay or said that I had to be gay to do the job.

Geri

"And that's why I'm home at..." Ellie looks at her watch. "At nine o'clock."

"No shit," says Geri.

"So if you folks don't mind, I'm going to bed," says Ellie.

"I'll come with you," says Geri. Everybody looks at Geri. "To talk. Just to talk."

*   *   *

Ellie is in bed, under the blankets. Geri is sitting on the side of the bed. "You know," they say, "I don't have a penis yet."

"I'm sorry," says Ellie. "We've done such a good job of maintaining our platonic relationship. I mean, I miss being physical with you..."

"As I do with you."

"But I don't want to act on my feelings. Not with a penis coming down the pipe."

*   *   *

In the living room, Jorge asks Krystal, "I was wondering, are you gay?"

"How do you mean?"

"You are a woman, no disputing that. But right now, you have a penis, which you will get removed. So do you date men or women? In other words, are you gay?"

"Good question," says Krystal. "I don't have sex now, so I guess I am asexual."

Geri steps into the living room just as the phone rings.

"You two really did nothing but talk?" Jorge asks Geri.

Krystal answers the phone. "This is she... Oh, hello Jason... Really? You did? So now what? Will they meet with me? I don't care if their lawyer has to be in the room... I'd like you to be in the room too, and my buddy, Geri, for moral support... Can you make it happen? In a couple of days? Do let me know. Thanks." Krystal hangs up the phone.

"Jason?" says Geri.

Geri

"They caught them?" says Jorge.
"Couple of days and I might get to meet my muggers."

Chapter Four

Geri takes to the Klub de Komedy stage. They pull up their carpentry belt which has slipped below their hips, brush back their rainbow-streaked hair, place their hands to the sides of their deep-set eyes, and peer into the audience. They take a deep breath and begin.

"Doctors...

"With that word, I feel like I've said enough and that I can take a bow and go home. What more can one say? They get rich not knowing what is happening to us. You go to your GP and he says, 'Well, the good news is that you are breathing and that your heart is beating. So, I know you are alive. Beyond that, I'll have to send you to a specialist. That will be one hundred and fifty bucks.'

"The specialist sends you for tests. A week later, the results come back. 'The results are inconclusive,' the specialist says. 'That will be five hundred bucks and I'll have to send you to a different specialist...'

"Can you imagine a plumber getting away with that? 'Well, the good news is that your water is running. That is why there are leaks all over the house. But I don't know why there are leaks. I'll have to call in a specialist. That will be one hundred and fifty bucks.'

"The plumbing specialist comes in and verifies that you have leaks because you are all wet and your carpets are moldy, and says, 'We'll have to get your pipes x-rayed.' He takes them all out and brings them back a week later saying, 'The test results are inconclusive. 'That will be five hundred bucks.'

"This much doctors do know: you are going to die one day. When and of what, they haven't got a friggin' clue. And don't get me started on psychologists. Doctors of the head. 'We know you're crazy. We just don't know why. Or what to do about it. Here, have a pill. It will bloat you, give you headaches and nausea, cause erectile dysfunction, and... you will still be crazy.'"

Geri

Geri does ten more minutes of comedy to laughter and applause that barely registers with them, takes an exaggerated bow to more applause, and exits stage right.

*   *   *

The four friends are in the kitchen making breakfast, moving around each other almost balletically. Even Krystal seems *en pointe* as she swoops around the others pouring her coffee and filling her bowl with cereal and milk. Jorge is dressed rather shabbily, in faded jeans ripped in an unfashionable manner and a wrinkled t-shirt with food stains on his belly.

Minutes later, sitting in the living room eating, Geri looks up at Jorge. "You're not as dapper looking as usual. No work today?"

Jorge does not reply. He shoves a spoonful of Cheerios into his mouth.

"Oh my gosh," says Ellie. "You've lost your job."

Jorge continues to chew and swallows.

"No!" says Geri.

"Shit happens," says Jorge. He plops his empty bowl on the ottoman and picks up his mug of coffee.

"Why?" says Ellie.

"Because," says Jorge. "I'm not a salesman. Evidently, my sales were the lowest on the sales totem pole. When dealing with me, people would buy a shirt, but not a tie. Underwear but no socks. A jacket, but no pants. Or nothing at all. Go figure."

"But what about all the clothes you bought?" asks Geri.

"That minus my paycheck, I'm only in hock $250. And I'm supposed to meet Mark for coffee tonight."

*   *   *

Ellie is on the couch, laptop on her thighs as she pecks away at her play. Geri is beside her, writing stand-up comedy thoughts in their notebook. Krystal is in one of the chairs reading a book. She looks up and says to nobody in particular, "What a lovely evening."

Jorge walks in through the door.

36

Geri

"You mean it was a lovely evening," Geri says looking up as Jorge stands in the living room, facing his friends as if waiting for the onslaught. "Home kind of early," they say to Jorge.

"I'd seen the movie at the Revue."

Ellie looks up. "Spill," she says. "Reconstruct."

"There's nothing to reconstruct."

"He didn't show?" asks Krystal.

"Oh, he showed. He showed. And then he left."

"Without even saying hello?" Geri asks.

Jorge takes a seat on the chair. "Okay," he says, "I'll reconstruct the evening for you, starting at 'hello'."

Jorge: Hello, you must be Mark.

Mark: Hello, Jorge.

Jorge: Have a seat. Good to meet you. How are you?

Mark: Good. Good. You?

Jorge: Fine, thanks.

Mark: So tell me, before we began to chat about ourselves. Do you know William Hoist at KPMG? He just moved to your firm. He used to work in the audit department with me at Lindquist Avey.

Jorge: Funny you should say that. I left KPMG some time ago.

Mark: Ah, it's still on your profile.

Jorge: Yes, I've been meaning to update that.

Mark: Who are you with now?

Jorge: Fredrick's. Well, I was with Fredrick's.

Mark: Never heard of them. Small firm?

Jorge: Men's fashion. Retail sales.

Mark: But you were with them. Are you saying that you are unemployed?

Jorge: Well, technically speaking...

Mark: So your profile is a lie?

Jorge: Well...

Mark: In more ways than one.

Jorge: Meaning?

Mark: Your profile picture. Five years younger. Twenty pounds lighter. And you had hair.

Jorge: Well, everybody fudges a little bit. No?

Geri

Mark: I think I'll be going now.
Jorge: But we haven't even ordered coffee...

"And just like that, he left," says Jorge.
Ellie snaps her fingers. "Just like that."
"Well at least he was gay and I doubt that he was married!" says Jorge.

*　　*　　*

Jorge, Krystal, and Geri are sitting around the ottoman eating breakfast. Ellie is in bed fighting a cold by nursing a mug of tea with lemon and honey.

Jorge asks them, "When you two have your transgender operations, if you have it, Geri, will you sleep with women or men? Will you be trans-homosexual or trans-heterosexual?"

"Are those even terms?" Geri asks. "Or did you just make them up?"

"I might be trans-asexual," says Krystal. "I'm doing this for me, not for sex. But, to take your bait, I like women and don't think that will change. So once I don't have a penis, I will be trans-homosexual because I will be a woman who wants to be with women."

"But," says Jorge, "if you have a penis now and want to be with women, you are not physiologically gay, even if you are a woman, albeit not physically. So once your penis is removed, won't you want to be with men?"

"Well, I don't think... I mean why would... I don't know. Now you've got me so freakin' confused..." Krystal pauses, thinking it over. "You've blown my mind. I have to talk this through with my shrink."

"You've found one?" asks Geri. "You haven't said anything."

"The talks are kind of deep and private. But going well. You should see her. She can help you sort out who you are."

"Maybe," says Geri. "Give me her number."

"I'll give you her name but not her number. If you make an appointment with her yourself you have to pay. Go to your doctor and have her refer you. Then Medicare will cover the cost of you seeing the shrink."

"But I don't want to see my doctor. If I do, I'll get poked and prodded and told I should be doing this and that, or else whatever will happen."

"It's how the system works," says Krystal. "Somebody has to pay something to someone if you don't want to pay anything to anybody."

"Then the system is broken," says Geri. "And what if your shrink cures me?"

"Isn't that what you want?"

"Maybe a fixed Geri would be a less funny Geri."

"You'd have to work hard to be a less funny Geri," says Jorge.

"Thanks."

"What he means," says Krystal, "is that the unfunny you is the funny you. It's why people come to see you. If I'm at your show and there are new people there looking quizzical as you perform, I tell them: 'They're not funny. But they're not supposed to be funny. That's what's so funny about them.' And then they relax into your routine."

"That's not what I meant, but we'll let it stand," says Jorge.

"Let me see if I have this straight, no pun intended. I'm a not funny, non-binary, maybe transsexual, comedian who earns their living as a carpenter?"

"That about sums it up," says Jorge.

"Do you want her name?" asks Krystal.

*   *   *

After lunch, Jorge and Krystal are walking on the Lakeshore boardwalk by Lake Ontario, enjoying the sun and the spring warmth. Past Sunnyside Pool and the Sunnyside Café they see a black preacher in a black two-piece suit, jacket unbuttoned, without a tie, and top shirt button undone, preaching to a crowd of several dozen congregants and curious onlookers, many sitting on the park grass.

"Halleluiah! Halleluiah!" says the preacher. "I am here to tell you that God loves each and every one of you. You are all precious in His name."

Several people in the crowd shout "Amen!"

"I am here to tell you that if you confess your sins to Jesus and dedicate your lives to God, there will be rewards for you, here on earth and in Heaven when you leave this temporary state of being."

Krystal smiles at Jorge, who smiles back. "You or me," says Krystal.

"You, all the way," says Jorge. "I'll be hiding behind this tree."

"Coward," says Krystal over her shoulder as she pulls her rainbow-coloured facemask up off her chin and places it over her mouth and nose before heading towards the preacher. "Excuse me, my good man," she says pointing a finger at the preacher when he pauses for a breath.

"How may I help you?" asks the preacher looking at Krystal parading towards him in all her transgender glory.

"This is a public park, yes?" asks Krystal. The preacher nods. "Since we both have the right to speak out in a public park, we can shout over each other or we can be cooperative and take turns."

"You would like to address my congregation?" asks the preacher.

"I'd actually like to address you. But first," she says turning towards the crowd, "how many of you have had the coronavirus vaccine shot?" Everybody including the preacher flexes an arm. Krystal flexes an arm too and pulls her mask down over her chin. "I'd like to talk to you, but your congregation is more than welcome to listen in."

"But we'll be gentlemen about it and take turns speaking?" asks the preacher.

"Gentlepersons," Krystal corrects him. "But yes."

"Since I don't know why you are here, you go first."

Krystal gestures at the preacher. "Where are you from?"

"Windsor," says the preacher. "Moved to Toronto years ago to attend Bible school and stayed. God provided, glory be."

"And before Windsor, your family was from?"

"The east coast. Halifax to be exact."

"And if we go back farther?"

"You can go all the way back to the southern States."

"So you are a descendent of slaves who were from Africa?"

"What are you implying?" says the preacher. "I am a free man washed in the blood of the lamb."

"I have no doubt that you are free. Just wanted to ensure that I hve it right," says Krystal. "Your ancestors were enslaved by white men. Beaten. Tortured. Raped. By white men. And here you are, generations later, praising the God of the white men. The God who looked on and allowed so much evil to happen to your forebears. The God who in His book tells His chosen people how to tend and even impregnate slaves." Krystal pauses. The preacher says nothing. "Why in, well, God's name, would you worship this God, the God of your white oppressors?"

"And you are a man parading before my congregation as a woman."

"We can discuss gender next if you wish. But you are dodging my question."

"The God of Moses, Abraham, and David is the God of all."

"But he allows some who praise his name to abuse others who did not know him?"

"He moves in mysterious ways. He brought me here to these people who are thirsty for His Word."

"Are you saying that your ancestors had to be enslaved, beaten, and raped so that you could talk to this crowd today?"

"I am saying His ways are mysterious, and you are making a mockery of them."

"Trust me, I am not mocking you in any way. I am truly curious."

"You are a man dressed as a woman questioning me based on no knowledge of God's word or my beliefs and convictions."

"There we go again with the gender thing, as if that has anything to do with..."

"It is who you are and it makes a mockery of the Word from Adam and Eve on..."

"On to the flood when your God says, 'Well, I made a bollocks of it all. Time to wipe everyone out, including innocent children, and start over with a chosen few and a bunch of animals.'"

41

"You, sir, are an abomination. There is a place in Hell for racist heathens like you."

"Heathen yes. Racist no."

Jorge comes out from behind the tree and walks up to Krystal. He takes her by the arm and gives her a gentle tug.

"Be gone with you and your crude thoughts," shouts the preacher.

"Crude," sputters Krystal.

"Let's go, my dear," says Jorge tugging Krystal even more firmly. "It's a beautiful day and the sunshine is calling to us."

"Be gone. Keep on walking, all the way to Hell," the preacher shouts.

Krystal tries to turn around, but Jorge increases the firmness of his grip on her elbow. "You started it," Jorge says, "Be big about it and let him have the last word."

"One of them is a woman, not a fellow," somebody in the congregation shouts.

"They've seeded my congregation with their friends," says the preacher.

Both Jorge and Krystal turn to see who is coming to their defense.

"I've never met them. But I will say this. She is more Christian than you." The angry man walks away from the congregation and a few others follow him.

"Okay," Krystal smiles. "We can go now."

*   *   *

Geri is heading out for a late afternoon walk to clear the comedy writing cobwebs from their head. They run into Nadir at the front door coming home from work.

"Hello, Nadir."

"Hello, Geri. How are you and how goes the routine for Canada One? Nicely toned down, but as funny as ever?"

"It's going. It's going."

"Glad to hear it," says Nadir as he enters the house.

Geri

"It's going. I'm going," says Geri as they head off on their cobweb-clearing walk.

When Geri gets home from their walk, Krystal is sitting on the edge of a chair. Ellie is standing beside her, hugging her and stroking her back.

"What's going on?" asks Geri.

"The police called," says Ellie. "Krystal can speak to the muggers today."

"You have to come with me, Geri."

"When do we go?"

"We should have left five minutes ago."

"Take off your mask and put on flats. We're running."

Krystal strips off her mask, kicks off her heels, and slips into flats.

"Wow," says Ellie. "This must be important."

*   *   *

Jason leads Krystal and Geri into a yellow-walled room with a table in the middle of it. Three boys, mid-teens, are sitting on one side of the table. Their lawyer is sitting at one end. Jason motions to two chairs across from the boys for Krystal and Geri. He sits at the other end of the table, across from the lawyer.

"Now as I have explained to these chaps, Bruce, David, Garth, and their lawyer, Bellamy, you have agreed that if they meet with you, as they are doing now, you will ask us, the police, to not press charges." Jason clears his throat. "Boys, this is Krystal and her friend, Geri. Bruce and David snigger at the mention of 'her.'

"Boys," warns Bellamy.

"It's okay," says Krystal, as Geri glowers.

"You have the floor," says Jason to Krystal,

Krystal takes a deep breath. "I had what I wanted to say all worked out. But now that we're here..." She pauses, breathes in, and begins again. "Thank you for meeting with me. I guess what I want to say is that I'm different than you. A lot different. And that makes you laugh at me and attack me. But we live in a world of

43

differences. If you go around attacking everything different, you will be fighting for the rest of your lives. Maybe that's how you want to live, fighting. It's not how I want to live. But if you fight me, I will fight back. Even if I am destined to lose, I'll go down swinging." She unconsciously adjusts her wig as the boys slouch in their chairs, Bruce with a smirk on his face, David looking neutral and Garth looking down at the table.

"I'm not asking you to befriend me or even care about me. I'm asking you to care about yourselves. Instead of picking on a lady in heels, instead of picking on someone you think is weaker than you…" Krystal pauses again and inhales deeply as if looking for her second wind. "You don't know how strong I have to be to be who I am, to become who I will be." She rubs her nose, looking for words.

"Picking on somebody who looks to be weaker than you is the action of the weak. I am here to tell you to be strong. Not for my sake, but for your sake. You don't have to like me. In fact, you can continue to hate me, for whatever immature and misguided reasons you chose. But I am asking you to not fight me. You have no reason to fight me or to fight anybody different than you. No reason to fight. None what-so-ever."

Krystal exhales a breath she did not even know she was holding in. She turns to Jason. "That's all I have to say."

Jason waits a beat and then says, "Boys, anything you have to say?" The boys all look down at the table and say nothing. Jason gives them a minute to shuffle uncomfortably but they still say nothing. "Then based on our agreement with Krystal, you are free to go."

Their lawyer gets up and taps them each on the back. They get up and leave the room with him. Garth is the last one out. He pauses at the door, looks back briefly at Krystal, then leaves.

"I don't know if it will have any impact on them, but well spoken," says Jason.

"I still think you should have asked for charges to be laid," says Geri. "But you almost had me tearing up there."

Chapter Five

Geri takes to the Klub de Komedy stage. They pull up their carpentry belt which has slipped below their hips, brush back their rainbow-streaked hair, place their hands to the sides of their deep-set eyes, and peer into the audience. They take a deep breath and begin.

"Good evening ladies and gentlemen, and those of you out there who are neither. I have a friend writing a play, in fits and starts. I have a friend dating and working, in fits and starts. I have a friend learning to walk in heels, in fits and starts. I am performing comedy, in fits and starts.

"Why when things start does it feel like they don't fit? As if I'm pulling up a pair of underwear two sizes too small. It's not only my life and the life of my companions. Take the trans-pastor of a church in Mississauga. She started preaching a year ago, but when she confessed to the congregation that she was trans she evidently didn't fit. Bang..." Geri pulls their hammer out of their tool belt, twirls it like a gun, and slips it back into the belt. "Fired."

"You know when comedians say, 'I'm not making this up' they usually are. Well, folks, I wish I were making this up. I wish I were making up the reaction of much of the straight community to the LGBTQ-plus community. We don't want to sleep with straight folks. Hell, often we don't even want to socialize with you. We'll work with you if we have to, but I don't get it. You straight folks are freaking out like you would if a troop of monkeys climbed all over you.

"I know, I just called the LGBTQ-plus community a troop of monkeys, but the fact is we're going ape-shit over the reaction of straight folks to our existence. Maybe we ought to throw feces at you. Feces in the face. Now that would give you something to complain about.

"But what I really want to know, beyond all this heterosexual kerfuffle is this: what is a trans person doing working as a minister in the first place? Oh, I support her right to preach, if that's what she wants to do, but doesn't she know that the belief in God is behind most of the ill will coming her way specifically, and in the world generally?

"God. Now there's somebody I'd like to fling feces at."

Geri does fifteen more minutes of comedy to rounds of laughter, takes an exaggerated bow to great applause, which barely registers with them, and exits stage right.

*   *   *

Deepa knocks on the door of the first-floor flat. Geri answers. Deepa is dressed in a mauve dress, carrying a black leather purse.

"Evening," says Geri.

"I was wondering if anybody was home this evening," says Deepa.

"Ellie is at work. Jorge is at the library. And I'm not sure where Krystal is. Taking her heels out for a walk, I suspect. But I'm all yours."

"I have to go to a book club dinner in thirty minutes. Nadir just called. He has an HR emergency at the bank and has to work late. Armaan is eleven and in grade seven. He can take care of himself, we let him do so after school, but he should have a sitter in the evening, and it's too late to find one. If I go out, there won't be anybody home with him for many hours. Is there any way? We'll pay you, of course."

"You got us Wi-Fi when we had none," says Geri. "I'm just writing. I can write upstairs as well as I can write down here. No charge."

"Thank you so much," says Deepa. "I don't know how to repay you."

"I feel that I am repaying you. Which book are you talking about tonight?"

"Oscar Wilde's *The Picture of Dorian Gray*. Enjoyed it very much."

"Ah, you are going classic, with a good one."

Deepa calls upstairs to Armaan. "Geri will be coming up." Armaan cheers. "He really likes you," says Deepa.

46

"And I like him. He's a great kid."

Geri gets their notebook and heads up the steps. Armaan is playing a crash-bang-boom game on Nintendo. "You want in?" he asks Geri.

They toss their notebook on the living room coffee table. "Best out of three. And if I lose, we go best out of five."

Several hours later, Nadir comes home and finds Geri and Armaan snuggled together, asleep on the couch. He picks up Armaan and takes him into his bedroom. He comes back and gently shakes Geri's shoulder. They snort and wake up, then laugh at themselves.

"Deepa called me and said that you had stepped into the breach. Did you get your work done?"

"We got Nintendo done," they say. "Thought I could take him. I was so wrong."

"Thank you so much."

"Any time, at least for the next year. He soon won't need anybody to sit with him."

"But he will always be happy to have you. And by way of payment, I won't ask you how the bank comedy writing is going."

*   *   *

Geri gets downstairs to find Jorge and Krystal on the couch in the living room chatting with the TV on in the background. They look up.

"Out tonight?" asks Jorge.

"Babysitting, if you want to call Armaan a baby. How goes it with you folks?"

"Three miles in heels; barely a wobble," says Krystal. "Then coffee at the Diplomatico, and smooth sailing back."

"And I applied for a new job and chatted online with Ramon."

"But not necessarily in that order," says Krystal.

"We're meeting for coffee at the end of next week, and I have a job interview tomorrow."

"I thought he was too shy for you. A bit of a wallflower," says Geri.

"He's a math major at the University of Toronto, so we have numbers in common. He has three roommates, another thing in common. And he works part-time as a bartender."

"So you have booze in common," says Geri.

"What's the job interview for?" asks Krystal.

"Insurance sales rep."

"But you suck at sales, especially commission sales," says Geri.

"It's two weeks of paid training. After that, who gives a darn?"

"You're not selling insurance to me," says Krystal.

"Don't worry, I've got it all figured out."

"The date or the job?" asks Geri.

*   *   *

After breakfast the next morning, Ellie is sitting on the couch typing away at her computer. "This is so much fun."

"What is?" asks Geri, sitting in a chair across from Ellie, scribbling in their notebook.

"This. Sitting on the couch, pounding on the keyboard, making words, sentences, scenes, acts."

"Ah, writing your play. What's it about?" asks Geri.

"Something," says Ellie. "It's about something."

"Funny that, because I'm doing pretty much the same thing with pen and paper, and having no fun at all."

Ellie looks up. "No fun at all?" She begins to type again. "So much fun, this is."

*   *   *

Armaan comes home after school and pounds on the first-floor door, which Geri answers. Armaan is clearly in a panic. "Can you come down the street? A friend from school is being picked on, and if I try to stop it we'll both get pounded."

48

Ellie is right behind Geri. "Let's go," she says and pushes Geri out the door. They run down the street with Armaan and find his friend, Theo, a block away sitting under a tree on a lawn nursing a bleeding nose. There are no thugs in sight. Ellie pulls some tissue out of a pocket and helps Theo stem the bleeding.

"What happened?" asked Geri.

"We were skipping home," says Armaan. "These high school kids, from Saint David's, the Catholic school a couple of blocks away, stopped us and called us stupid faggots and queers. Theo said, 'So what if I am?' Because, well he is, but not stupid or an idiot. And they put a beating on him."

Geri and Ellie help Theo up. Other than the nose, which has all but stopped bleeding, he seems fine. They all walk back to Armaan's house, on the lookout for the students who attacked Theo, but see nobody.

At the front door, Armaan says, "I'd tell my folks, but my mom is out doing volunteer work and dad is at the bank."

"Want to stay down here and have some hot chocolate with us?" Geri asks.

"Thank you," says Armaan. Theo nods.

As Geri is making hot chocolate, Theo asks, "What's with guys like that?"

"This is small comfort, but Canada is one of the most LGBTQ-plus open and friendly countries in the world, including the legalization of gay marriage," Geri says. "LGBTQ-plus relationships are illegal in over seventy countries. In a dozen countries, being gay or bisexual is punishable by death."

He serves each of the boys a mug of hot chocolate. Theo and Armaan blow on their drinks to cool them.

"Are you saying that in Canada I can be beaten up because I'm gay," says Theo, "but I can marry the man of my dreams?"

Geri takes a deep breath. "I guess that about sums it up."

*   *   *

The next day, after breakfast, Ellie says to Geri, "We should go to the Catholic high school and let the principal know what

49

happened. They might not be able to catch the students who hit Theo, but they should be able to do something. Don't you think?"

"Like hold an assembly and talk to all the students."

"Like hold an assembly and have *you* talk to all the students."

Geri and Ellie go to Saint David's to speak to the principal, Mr. Ryan. He invites them to take seats in his office and they explain what happened. He says that there is nothing much he can do about such situations when they happen off school property.

Geri asks him what the school's LGBTQ-plus policy is and the principal becomes flustered. "Technically, we don't have one," Mr. Ryan says.

"Well, you have a choice," Ellie says. "Develop one and announce it at an assembly for your students that you are going to hold, introducing Geri as a guest speaker. Public speaking is what he does. Or we call the police and bring Theo and Armaan room to room until we find the thugs."

Mr. Ryan leans back in his seat, looking concerned. A few awkward moments go by before he speaks. "I see that you have a real concern here, and your assembly suggestion is a good one. I'll have to speak to my administrative staff about this, but I can assure you that we will address the issue. And we are overdue for a formal, written LGBTQ-plus policy."

The next day, Mr. Ryan calls Geri and Ellie with a date and time for the student assembly. The principal promises to unveil an LGBTQ-plus policy at the assembly, before Geri addresses the students.

A week later, Theo and Armaan, both sets of their parents, and Geri and Ellie are on the assembly hall stage in front of students and teachers who fill the hall for the unveiling of the school's new LGBTQ-plus policy.

Standing behind a podium, Mr. Ryan introduces those on the stage with him to the audience. He tells those assembled that Theo was beaten up by students from the school because he is gay. He says such action cannot be tolerated by the school or the community. He then reads the school's new policy in support of the LGBTQ-plus community, a statement that hits all the right notes in its supportive and inclusive content. He tells students that the LGBTQ-plus policy will be posted in the office, cafeteria, and each classroom. He then asks Geri to say a few words to the assembled students and teachers.

Geri gets up and walks to the centre of the stage, ignoring the podium.

"Good afternoon, and thanks for inviting me to speak today," Geris says. "I am a non-binary person, neither male nor female, as I suspect a few of you may be. Ellie here is gay, as is Theo, the boy who was beaten up recently by students from your school because he is different than some of you. We are part of the LGBTQ-plus community--lesbian, gay, bisexual, transgender, and queer or questioning." They clear their throat.

"Over five percent of the Canadian population identify as LGBTQ-plus. Over eleven percent aged eighteen to thirty-four identify as LGBTQ-plus." Geri pauses for a moment as many people in the audience whisper and look around. "There are about seven hundred people in the auditorium today," they continue. "That means there are over seventy LGBTQ-plus people here, even if some of you do not yet know that that is who you are."

There is an audible gasp in the audience.

"I know," Geri responds to the gasp and gestures to the audience. "We have a lot of allies out there. But don't worry. I am not going to ask you to stand up and identify yourselves. However, I am going to tell the rest of you that a heck of a lot of people are different in their sexual orientation than you are." Gerry clears their throat.

"In addition, the rest of you are different from each other. Some of you are male, some female, and some, as I said, non-binary. Some short, some tall, some average height. Some fat, some skinny, some average weight. Some have brown hair, some black, some blonde, and some red. Heck, I can even see a number of you with purple hair and some with various colours of streaks in your hair, as I have." This gets a laugh. "My point is, who among you is not different? If you are not in any way different than your classmates, put up your hands." They wait a beat. Not a hand goes up.

Geri

"That's all I'm saying folks. If you want to beat up somebody for being different, you have to start with the person beside you, unless they get to you first, because we are all different. Celebrate your differences and those of the people around you and you will make this a more joyful and inclusive school, and will help make it a more joyful and inclusive world."

Geri takes a slight bow to a solid round of applause and exits stage right. Theo, Armaan, their parents, and Ellie follow them off-stage.

*   *   *

Walking home together, Armaan says, "I really liked what you said."

Theo adds, "I don't know if it will make any difference. I mean assholes are assholes..."

"Theo!" his mother shouts, then laughs, "But we get what you mean."

"...but it had to be said, and they had to hear it."

"It was lovely," says Deepa.

"You even got a laugh," Nadir points out.

"That's what you focused on?" asks Geri with a chuckle.

"Of course. After all, you're my man, er, person." And they all laugh.

*   *   *

A few days later, over breakfast, Jorge stands up, with a bowl of Cheerios in his hand, to make an announcement. "Gather around my friends. I have some news."

Geri looks at Ellie who is on the couch with them. Ellie looks at Krystal in the chair across from her.

"If we were gathered any closer," says Geri, "we'd be up your nose."

Krystal chokes back his coffee. Ellie almost spits up a mouthful of Raisin Bran.

"Just listen up then," says Jorge. "I landed the new job, as an insurance agent in training."

"As I said, you're not going to sell me insurance," says Krystal.

"I won't be selling anybody any policies," Jorge says. "It's two weeks of salaried training. Once my paycheque is deposited, I hand in my resignation."

"Isn't that kind of, I don't know, unethical?" asks Ellie. "I mean won't the insurance company be pissed off losing money on you?'

"Are you kidding? Nothing insurance companies do loses them money. Remember, I'm an accountant."

"Pray tell, how do they make money by you quitting?" asks Geri.

"If you really want to know..."

"I don't. But go ahead."

"Everything is planned. They know how many trainees they have and how many will sell policies to friends and family during the training period. That covers the cost of training us, even the losers like me. In other words, they expect there to be a couple of losers with zero sales in each group. I am one of the zero-sales trainees."

"But no trainee goes into training expecting to crap out," says Ellie.

"Who cares? The numbers indicate how many trainees will sell, how much they'll sell, and how many will crap out. The course is set up on a cost-recovery basis."

"Seems like a bit of a crap shoot," says Krystal.

"It's all a crap shoot, but not for the insurance company. They make money on everything." He sits and wolfs down some Cheerios, then says, "Say you buy term insurance that expires when you hit sixty-five. Do you know why the premiums go up every few years?"

"They do?" asks Krystal.

"Indeed," says Jorge. "Every few years people are closer to death, according to the actuarial tables, so up go the premiums. But what happens if you hit sixty-five and don't die?" The friends all shake their heads. "The policy expires and you get nothing. What you've paid in is pure profit for the insurance companies."

"But some people die before sixty-five," says Ellie.

"The actuarial tables take that into account and the premiums are set to cover the payouts for death, while still turning a tidy profit for the insurance companies." Jorge chews back more cereal. "Die before the actuarial tables say you should, and your family reaps the benefit. Don't die and you get nothing. The insurance companies price each type of policy according to their need to turn a profit. Two weeks' pay, then I look for another job, and I don't feel the least bit unethical about it. In the meantime, I have a date with Ramon coming up in a couple of days."

*   *   *

Krystal brings a newspaper home that evening and is so distraught she can barely speak.

"You can gather all you need to know online, now that we have Wi-Fi," says Geri. "Now we're going to have to remember to recycle that."

Krystal slaps the paper down on the ottoman and points to a headline. Geri, Ellie, and Jorge lean in to look and see what Krystal is pointing at in large type on the front page: "Trans pastor fired for coming out to Mississauga congregation."

Krystal pulls the newspaper back. "Here, let me read you a bit." She begins to read.

On Monday, 127 members of the Lorne Park Baptist Church in Mississauga, Ontario, voted 62 to 55 to fire Ms. Junita Joplin, who has been their pastor for a year. 'I came out as transgender in June, and I got fired in July,' Ms. Joplin said.

'There are a lot of good people in that congregation who stuck by me and stuck their necks out to support me. To no avail,' she added.

The church said that the vote came after a month of 'prayerful discussions' between the reverend and the congregation.

'Up until June 14, I was perceived as male, as Jules,' Joplin said.

During the sermon in which she came out, she told the congregation, 'I am not just supposed to be a pastor: I'm also supposed to be a woman. My name is not Jules. I am Junita. I am transgender. I am she and I am having a sex-change operation because I want to be the person that God meant me to be.'"

"She is me," says Krystal. "We have to do something. On Sunday, we have to protest outside the church."
"Protest?" asks Geri. "The fact that she was fired or the fact that she believes there is a God?"
"We may not believe in her belief, but she has every right to be wrong about it, and every right to keep her job," says Krystal.
"Krystal is right," says Ellie.
"So right," says Jorge.
"We go down to the Village tonight and round up troops for Sunday," says Krystal.

*   *   *

On Sunday, the four friends and several dozen other protesters are outside the Mississauga church carrying rainbow-coloured signs that say 'Restore the Pastor' and 'Let Junita Preach'. They march peacefully in front of the church. As they march they shout, "Let Junita preach. Let Junita preach." Krystal leads the march. She has on her best heels, as do other marchers from the trans community. The protestors stop every couple of minutes and let congregants peacefully pass through their ranks and into the church in ones and twos or family groups.
After the protesters have been marching and shouting for ten minutes, five police cars show up and ten cops exit the cars. They have batons in hand.
"We're in for it now," Jorge says to Geri.
"Just stay tight," says Ellie.
A cop comes up to Krystal leading the parade of protestors. They chat back and forth for several minutes. No congregants pass while they are talking.
Krystal turns and addresses the marchers. "It seems we are an illegal protest. We haven't filled out any paperwork." The protestors mumble amongst themselves. "Since we've been so peaceful, they

will give us another five minutes. Then we have to disperse, or else..." Krystal looks over the group she is leading. "I don't know about you, and if anybody wants to leave, I fully understand. But I vote for 'or else.'"

There are cheers as the protesters start to march and chant again.

They loop around in front of the church doors several times when a woman wearing a flowing brunette wig and a black pulpit gown sweeping the ground appears before them. "My friends," she shouts, "may I speak with you for a moment?"

Krystal puts up a hand to stop the march. "Junita!" she shouts. "It's Junita."

"Thank you, madam," says Junita.

Krystal nods her head and gestures toward Junita. "The pulpit is all yours."

Junita clears her throat. "I want you to know that I love that you are here, and why you are here. God loves you for being here too. But the congregation, not God, has spoken. They took a legal vote and made a binding decision, one that I respect. I don't agree with it, but I respect it."

"They can reverse it," shouts Krystal to cheers from the protestors.

"That would make me the pastor of a church in which more than half of the congregation doesn't want me," says Junita. "That is not God's will for me. I shall find another congregation that will embrace me, as you have, for who I am. I will be upfront with that congregation about who I am. There will be no deception. There will be only acceptance."

"Amen! Hallelujah!" shout members of the protest.

"But," says Junita with a smile, "since you've come this far to support me, allow me to walk with you. Three times around--for God the Father, God the Son, and God the Holy Spirit--and then we go."

Junita links arms with Krystal at the head of the protest.

"Junita will preach again," Krystal shouts, pumping a fist in the air.

"Junita will preach again," the protestors reply, pumping fists in the air. They march and shout, "Junita will preach again." Three times around they go and then follow Junita and Krystal, still locked arm in arm, off the church property.

The cops shake their heads in disbelief, get back into their cars, and drive away.

Junita looks down at Krystal's shoes. "Fabulous heels," she says. "Fab-u-lous. You wear them well."

"I wore them just for you!"

When they get home, Krystal says, "I could use a beer."

"Beer," calls Ellie.

"Way more beer," says Jorge.

"We couldn't afford any more beer," says Geri. "How about glasses of water all around?"

*   *   *

A few days later, after dinner, Jorge says, "Tonight's the night. I go on a date with Ramon. Third time lucky, as they say."

"What's on at the Revue tonight?" asks Geri.

"Cynic," says Jorge. He hesitates, then says, "Retro night. Bogart and Bacall. The Big Sleep."

"I should be back from work by the time The Big Sleep lets out," says Ellie.

"And I'll be back from the Village by then," adds Krystal.

"And I'll be right here, writing, or watching TV," says Geri. "Speaking of writing," they say to Ellie, "you don't mind if I use the laptop while you're at work?"

"Not at all," she says, and adds, "My play file is password protected."

"Nuts," mutters Geri.

"I'm off to shower, then I'm off," says Jorge.

*   *   *

Geri

Ellie is on the couch, typing away at her play. Geri is beside her, writing comedy thoughts in their notebook. Krystal is in one of the chairs reading a book. She looks up and says to nobody in particular, "What a lovely evening. Although it feels familiar."

"It kind of does," says Geri.

Ellie looks up from her keyboard. "It does, kind of." She resumes typing.

Jorge walks in the door.

"You mean it was a lovely evening," Geri says. "How was The Big Sleep?" they ask Jorge.

"IMDB doesn't give it an eight out of ten for no reason."

Ellie stops typing and looks up. "Spill," she says. "Details. Reconstruct your night."

"He showed up at the café?" asks Krystal.

"And left when?" asks Geri.

"Oh, he showed. And he left... when the movie ended." Jorge takes a seat on the chair. "I'll reconstruct the café evening for you, from when the strudel with whipping cream and coffee arrives."

Jorge: Their strudel with whipping cream is divine.

Ramon: Looks delicious.

Jorge: So, tell me about yourself, beyond your profile. Any updates on who you are and what you are doing?

Ramon: Well, the university term has ended. I'm working full-time as a bartender now, with one more year to go in the Master's program. Then I guess I will officially be a mathematician, still working as a bartender though, I presume.

Jorge: Ah, you need to be more optimistic. I'm trained in accounting and am now selling insurance.

Ramon: That's new.

Jorge: I suppose I should update my profile.

Ramon: I like that you are selling insurance because I've been thinking about buying.

Jorge: And here I thought you'd be afraid I was going to try to sell you, which I'm not.

Ramon: Perhaps you can answer my questions. But I have to tell you something about me that is not on my profile.

Jorge: I'm all ears, even as I dig into my strudel.

Ramon: This is difficult to say. You see, before I came out I had a girlfriend, Maggie.

Jorge: Many of us had girlfriends in our closeted pasts.

Ramon: But most of us did not get our girlfriends pregnant. Most of us don't have a son. Her parents help Maggie with Henry as she continues her studies. Maggie and I, we are still friends. She was very understanding about me coming to terms with my sexual orientation.

Jorge: You have... a son?

Ramon: That is not a deal breaker, is it? It was two years ago, before I came out.

Jorge: Not a deal breaker. Just a bit of a surprise is all.

Ramon: I help out with what I can. But I thought I should get insurance, in case something happens to me.

Jorge: Crapshoot.

Ramon: Pardon?

Jorge: Insurance. Crapshoot.

Ramon: That raises about twenty questions. I'm just wondering if you can tell me the best policy to buy, under my circumstances.

Jorge: Insurance companies plan on you living a good, long life, as most of us do according to the actuarial tables. Say you get a one hundred thousand dollar term policy that ends when you turn sixty-five. Your payments average one hundred and fifty dollars a month for forty years or seventy-two thousand dollars in premiums by the time you're sixty-five. Because you want to contribute to Henry's life as well, you give Maggie the same amount until you're sixty-five. That's one hundred and forty-four thousand dollars spent, but Henry only gets half."

Ramon: But what if I die before I'm sixty-five?

Jorge: That's the crapshoot. The actuarial tables say you most likely will not. At sixty-five, the term policy ends and the insurance company keeps your money. Give Henry what you can, while you can, for as long as you can."

Ramon: I don't know...

Jorge: What would Maggie say if you told her you'd like to give her one hundred and fifty dollars a month now to help with Henry, and that you'd increase the amount when you can?
Ramon: She would be ecstatic...
Jorge: Then make her so! And forget about insurance.
Ramon: What are you doing after dessert?
Jorge: I was going to see The Big Sleep at the Revue.
Ramon: Bogart and Bacall. I love them.
Jorge: If you'd care to join me...

"And," says Jorge to his friends, "he joined me, and we loved the movie."
"Yowza," says Krystal. "Quite the night."
"Third time lucky indeed," says Geri.
"So," asks Ellie, "when do you see him again?"
"Sometime next week."

*   *   *

Over a breakfast of orange juice and poached eggs, Krystal says, "If I am going to start hormone therapy and have the transgender operation, my psychologist, Natalie Harmon, says I need to be in shape."
"You look pretty good," says Jorge as he chews on his Cheerios.
"Weight is almost in ratio to height," says Krystal, "but I have to lose a couple of pounds and boost my cardio. I've started a new diet and have signed up at a women's fitness club."
"Aren't fitness clubs expensive?" asks Ellie as she blows on her coffee to cool it down.
Krystal scoops egg off her plate. "The one I joined gives you your first month free." She lifts a forkful of egg towards her mouth. "A lot of them do. I'll move from club to club and see how it goes." She shoves egg into her mouth and starts to chew.
"Brilliant," says Geri. "Jorge has a job that pays him to not sell insurance. You won't pay to get in shape. Now all we need is a playwright who sells tickets to plays that other people write, and a

comedian who sells their soul to pay the rent... Wait, we already have that. We are the perfect trifecta."

"Trifectas come in three," says Ellie.

"Okay then, the imperfect trifecta."

"In a couple of days," says Jorge, "you three will be the trifecta. I'll be unemployed."

"I hear Costco is hiring cashiers," says Krystal.

"Me, stand in front of a cash register and swipe goods that make it beep, all while not using my brain? Where do I sign up?"

Chapter Six

Geri takes to the Klub de Komedy stage. They pull up their carpentry belt which has slipped below their hips, brush back their rainbow-streaked hair, place their hands to the sides of their deep-set eyes, and peer into the audience. They take a deep breath and begin.

"What I'd like to know is this: Why can't people get along? I mean I know why racists can't get along with people of colour. It's because the racists are goddamn, freakin', ignorant idiots. Just in case you were wondering.

"And I know why fundamentalist Christians hate members of the LGBTQ-plus community. There is a verse in Leviticus, a book in the Old Testament for those of you not up on your Bible studies. Leviticus chapter eighteen verse twenty-two: 'You shall not lie with a male as with a woman; it is an abomination.'

"Mind you, there are verses in Leviticus that condemn seventy-five other things. I don't want to stand up here and accuse fundamentalists of cherry-picking, but I will pick a cherry for them.

"Do you know that there are verses that condemn the eating of blood and eating any seafood without fins or scales? I'm just saying that any Christian who likes his surf 'n turf rare with shrimp will be joining his LGBTQ-plus brothers and sisters in Hell. At least according to Leviticus."

This draws a laugh.

"But when it comes to LGBTQ-plus brothers and sisters you'd think there'd be a little more tolerance towards each other. And overall, there is. But sometimes...

"However, I see by the flashing white light out there that I am running out of time tonight because we have a jammed-packed lineup of comedians who are actually funny, so we'll have to save that one."

Geri takes an exaggerated bow to applause and exits stage right.

Geri

*   *   *

Over breakfast, Jorge makes a grand announcement. "The Eagle has landed. Landed at Costco with a job as a cashier."

Geri, Ellie, and Krystal cheer.

"And," Jorge continues, "I have a second date lined up with Ramon."

Geri, Ellie, and Krystal cheer again.

"And I," announces Krystal, "will be going to Femmes, the fitness club, for a workout and then a sauna."

Geri, Ellie, and Jorge cheer.

"And I have completed the first draft of my play," Ellie says. "Still needs tweaking and fine-tuning, but draft one she is done."

Geri, Krystal, and Jorge cheer.

"And I..." Geri says. "I got nothing."

*   *   *

After breakfast, Geri leaves for a carpentry job. Ellie asks Jorge and Krystal if they have some time to listen to her read her play. "I have to read it aloud before working on the next draft. Reading it aloud helps me hear the voice of the play. And that will help me tweak it."

"What about Geri?" asks Krystal.

"I'd like to hear what you two think first."

"Time I have today," says Jorge. "Tomorrow I start training to wave products in front of the scanner at Costco."

"Count me in," says Krystal. "I'm going to the club for a workout and a sauna, but not until after lunch. As a free member, the hours I can use the club are restricted to non-rush hour times, like after lunch, and I have to be out by three o'clock. That kind of thing."

"Okay then," says Ellie. She begins to read. She reads for over an hour. Jorge and Krystal laugh and cry and punch their fists in the air.

"Curtain," Ellie says as she comes to the end of the play.

63

Jorge and Krystal leap to their feet and applaud. "You're giving that to a producer at the theatre company," Jorge says.

"Today, if not sooner," Krystal chimes in.

"No tweaking," says Jorge. "Just give it to people who matter."

Ellie shakes her head as if she can't believe what she is hearing. "No tweaking, you say?"

"Just giving," says Jorge.

"Damn. I just might do that."

*   *   *

Krystal is at the women's club. She lifts some light weights then speed-walks the treadmill and works up a good sweat. After her walk, she strips down in the changing room, wraps a towel around her waist, and heads for the sauna. She opens the sauna door and takes a deep breath of moist, hot air. "Ah," she sighs. "My kind of atmosphere."

Two young women, Joan and Jenny, are sitting naked on a bench behind the hot stones, ladling water onto them. Steam hisses into the air.

"Hello ladies," says Krystal. "The more steam the merrier." She sits on the bench across from the women and strips off her towel.

The women look at her, and then at each other. They chat quietly and then Joan looks up at Krystal. "You do know this is a ladies club," she says.

"That's why I'm here," Krystal replies with a smile meant to disarm.

"But," Joan continues, "you have what is commonly known as a penis or prick."

"I'm transgender," says Krystal. "The operation hasn't been scheduled yet."

"Then you are a man with a dick in the sauna of a women's club," says Joan.

"Beg to differ," says Krystal, "but I am a woman born with a penis, who is working out and taking a sauna to get in shape and lose weight so that I can have it removed."

"You still have a freakin' penis," says Jenny.

"It will be gone in a year or so."

"Until then, you shouldn't be naked in the sauna in a women's club," says Joan.

"When I joined the club, I asked about the sauna rules. Rule number one is 'No men in the sauna.' No men, not no penises. The penis is just there for now. It's not like I have any desire to use it, other than to urinate from it, and if I have to pee I promise you that I will leave."

"Well if you are not covering up or getting the hell out of here, then we are. Come on, Jenny."

The women wrap themselves in their towels, take each other by the hand, and head for the door. Jenny turns back to Krystal. "Trust me, we will be asking management for a firm and quick ruling on this."

*   *   *

That evening over dinner, Krystal tells her friends what transpired in the sauna. "The thing is, the women who complained were gay. I thought gay women would be allies."

"Some gay women get freaky over penises," says Ellie. "No matter to whom they are appended."

"Management has already talked to me. There will be a meeting in a couple of days. Until then, I'm banned from the sauna. Me. Banned."

"Do you need a lawyer?" Geri asks.

"I know a legal secretary," says Ellie.

"I wouldn't be able to afford a lawyer or even a legal secretary. I'm just going to roll with the ruling."

"Do I see another protest coming up?" asks Jorge.

"Not if I win," laughs Krystal.

"When," says Geri. "When you win."

*   *   *

The next day, Jorge is at his first Costco training session, behind the cash register with his young, pimply-faced trainer,

Marcus. They work together for a couple of hours cashing out customers with Marcus showing Jorge how to swipe product over the barcode reader and showing him which buttons to press, and when to press them, on the cash register. Then they go on a coffee break.

During the break, Jorge says, "I think I'm getting the hang of it. If you don't mind I'd like to ask you a few questions to make sure that I'm on track."

Marcus nods and lifts a cardboard coffee cup to his lips.

"So what I basically have to do," Jorge says, "is swipe the product barcode over the barcode scanner. It reads the price and sends it to the cash register. I press the Total button and the cash register totals the bill, including tax. I don't have to know which products are taxed and which are not?"

Marcus nods again. "Yep."

"I don't have to pack any bags. If the client pays cash, I make change. I key in the amount the customer has given me and the cash register tells me how much change to give the customer. However, as we saw this morning, most customers swipe their debit or credit card over the card reader after the bill has been totaled. If there are any problems at all, including any price disputes, I call the help number and a manager will sort out the issue?"

"Sounds like you've got it," says Marcus.

Jorge cracks his knuckles. "Then I'm set. Let's get back out there!"

"But we still have eight minutes left on our break."

"Then I'm getting a donut!" says Jorge.

*　*　*

A few days after he starts his new job at Costco, Jorge has a second date with Ramon.

Ramon says that he and Maggie talked over insurance versus financial contributions to his son's upbringing. "She, like you, thought insurance was silly, but for a different reason. 'It will bring death on,' she says. She is happy to accept a modest financial contribution as long as I have a few bucks to spare. She also said that I should start to see Henry more formally. It kind of took me by surprise, but Maggie and I get along and I love Henry. I think it's just taken us time to work out who we are to each other, and to Henry."

"That is very cool," said Jorge. "Will you be visiting Henry as the dad or a friend of the family? Also, at some point, no rush, do I get to meet him?"

Ramon blushes. "Yes, to the second question. As the dad, to the first. Even when Maggie dates someone new, she feels it is important for Henry to know his real dad.

"Maggie sounds like a sweet, intelligent person," says Jorge.

"If I wasn't gay..." says Ramon with a chuckle.

*   *   *

The next night that Ellie goes to work, she takes a USB stick with her play on it. Before her box office work begins, she knocks on the cubicle wall of Jane Petron, Rainbow Theatre's artistic director. "Come in, Ellie," Jane says. "What can I do for you?"

Ellie enters a bit sheepishly and explains that she has written a play. "It's an early draft, but I was wondering if you might, no rush, be willing to take a look at it and give me some feedback or tell me if it sucks."

Jane laughs. "Leave it with me. It may be a while before I get to it, and if it sucks, I will tell you. But I'll do so in such a constructive manner that you will think you're close to genius."

"Here is the USB key," says Ellie. "And thanks so much for this."

*   *   *

Just after breakfast, Krystal receives a call from Mazy Dagon, the manager of Femmes, telling her that they have created a formal sauna policy and asking her if she can come in for a meeting.

"I can be there in fifteen minutes," says Krystal.

"We were thinking more like two o'clock," says Mazy.

Geri

At two p.m. sharp, Krystal knocks on Mazy's office door. "Come in," says Mazy.

Krystal enters to see Mazy, Joan, and Jenny sitting around Mazy's desk. Mazy gestures to an empty chair beside Joan. "Okay," she says, "now that we're all here, I will proceed."

Joan and Jenny don't look at Krystal as Mazy continues, "After receiving a formal complaint about penises in the sauna from Joan and Jenny, I conducted a survey of our members and met with our club lawyer." She pauses and looks at the women across from her. "I want you to know that we took this issue seriously and have reached a final and binding decision."

Krystal looks at Joan and Jenny who still won't look in her direction. "They already know?" asks Krystal.

Mazy shakes her head. "They got here just before you did. I wanted you all here at the same time so that you can hear the new policy and ask any questions you may have."

"And?" says Krystal, like somebody asking for a band-aid to be ripped off a wound.

"This is a club exclusively for women. Members who are transgender women, be they pre-op or post-op, are women. Pre-op they have penises. Members are allowed to use all our facilities, including the sauna. So a pre-op transgender woman can use the sauna and, like any other member, can be naked in the sauna."

"Thank you," says Krystal. "Your ruling makes so much sense."

"Members," says Marcy. "Unfortunately, you are not a formal member of Femmes. Should you choose to join the club, the policy will apply to you."

"But," says Krystal, "that's a double standard for women."

"No," says Marcie, "it's a different standard for members and trial members. Just like you can't use the club during rush hours you can't be naked in the sauna."

"Does this policy works for you?" Krystal asks Joan and Jenny.

Joan looks at Jenny who nods. "We'll agree to it," says Joan. "If you formally join Femmes and enter the sauna when we're in it, we can leave if we don't want to deal with..." She drifts off.

"So that is the new policy," says Marcy.

"I won," says Krystal. "But somehow I also lost."

Geri

* * *

Geri knocks on the door to the second floor. Armaan comes down the steps and answers. "Is your dad home," Geri asks. Armaan nods. "Can you ask him if he has a moment to see me?" Armaan runs up the stairs. A few minutes later Nadir comes down.

"Geri, how are you?" he asks.

"I've been better."

"Do tell."

"I can't do it. The comedy gig for your bank. I've tried to write it but I keep on drawing blanks."

Nadir strokes his chin several times. "You know that you signed a contract?"

"I know."

"And you know that your rent is overdue?"

"I know."

"And you know that you did not ask me if your friends could move in."

"I know."

"I tell you what..."

"I know..."

"No, you don't know. I will let you out of your contract. I will have no problems with your friends being here. I will not even change the Wi-Fi password. And I will give you another two weeks to pay your rent."

Geri clasps their hands together in thanks. "What will you do for your event?" they ask.

"I've heard of a comic who does gay humour that is going over well and will contact him. Do you know Robert Sorbain?"

"Robert Sorbain? Do I know him? That's who you're thinking of getting? Freak it. I'll do the gig. Just keep Sorbain off your stage."

Nadir shakes his head, "But I thought..."

"I'm in. I'm doing it."

"As you wish," says Nadir. "You are our first choice. Well, second choice. But you know what I mean."

Chapter Seven

Geri takes to the Klub de Komedy stage. They pull up their carpentry belt which has slipped below their hips, brush back their rainbow-streaked hair, place their hands to the sides of their deep-set eyes, and peer into the audience. They take a deep breath and begin.

"Welcome to Pride Month. The Pride Parade is four weeks away." There is great applause and riotous cheers that Geri actually hears. "I should open every routine with that"

To that there is laughter.

"I mean can you imagine taking the stage in November and saying, 'Welcome to Pride Month. The Pride Parade is four weeks away.' People would go crazy. Or think that I was crazy. Either way, I'd get a reaction!"

Geri does twenty more minutes of comedy to almost non-stop laughter that they barely hear, takes an exaggerated bow to great applause, and exits stage right.

They go backstage where they meet Gaston loosening up his vocal cords. Geri notices some white powder on the end of Gaston's nose and says, "You might want to wipe your nose before you go out there."

Gaston rubs the end of his nose, looks at his fingers, and licks the powder on them. "I don't know how you do it."

"Do what?'

"Go out there night after night, sober, and bare your soul to them. Don't your insides get eaten alive while you are out there?"

"Doing cocaine before I go on would help, how?"

"Instead of being eaten alive, you would feel alive," Gaston says.

Geri pauses for a moment. "Maybe before my next show. It wouldn't hurt to try. I don't know. What would it cost me?"

"It costs you your soul. But it's well worth it."

"I meant dollars and cents."

Geri

"Tell you what. You want to try it before your next gig? I'll give you one bump for free. And then you decide."

*   *   *

Jorge and Ellie are at work. Krystal has headed downtown to do a little window shopping before she goes clubbing. Geri is writing, actually using Ellie's laptop, when there is a knock on the door. They plop the laptop on the couch, close the lid, and get up to answer the door.

Armaan asks, "May I come in?"

"Of course," says Geri with a bow. "Enter. You are always welcome here." Armaan laughs and enters. He sits on a chair across from the couch. Geri sits back down on the couch. "So," they say, "what can we do for you?'

Armaan hesitates for a moment. He bites his knuckles on one hand.

"Flesh-eating. Must be important," says Geri.

"You remember my friend Theo?" Armaan asks.

"Will never forget him."

"He's a really sweet guy, and he is gay, and I like him..." Armaan shifts in the chair.

Geri nods encouragingly.

"Does my liking him make me gay too?"

"Not at all," Geri says. "There are people who like me and that doesn't make them non-gender. People who like Krystal are not necessarily transgender. And some people are not gay but they are friends with Ellie and even with Jorge."

"But what if I really like him?"

"It all depends on what you mean by 'really' and 'like'. Many feelings change over time. For instance, Jorge is dating Ramon and Ramon has a son. So at one time, Ramon was with a woman. But now he's gay." Geri opens the laptop. "Since we have Wi-Fi, thank you very much for that, would you like to take a sexual orientation quiz online?"

"I guess so," says Ramon.

"I have a couple bookmarked. You can take them and I'll sit with you in case you need any of the questions explained."

Geri opens their browser and clicks on a link in favourites. They pat a cushion on the couch. Armaan scoots over. "Here," says Geri handing him the laptop. Armaan takes it and works his way through a series of multiple-choice questions. The final result is displayed on the screen.

Armaan reads the results: "Heterosexual. Gay friendly."

"In other words, cool dude," says Geri. "Want to try another one?"

"Sure."

Geri takes back the laptop and looks for the next quiz in their list of favourites. They hand the laptop back to Armaan who answers another set of multiple-choice questions. He hits enter at the end of the quiz.

"And the winner is..." The results appear on the screen. "Heterosexual. Gay curious," Armaan reads.

"There you be," says Geri. "You're the best kind of hetero a gay person could know."

Armaan smiles. "That sounds like me. I'm happy, not gay."

"Sums it up nicely."

"And my folks too, you know?"

"They are sweet people, your mom and dad, and have been very friendly toward the LGBTQ-plus community."

"They know a lot of idiots."

"There are people like you and your folks and there are people like the kids who beat up Theo. I don't know why, but there is such a difference between people."

"My dad says back home, where we're from, he had a gay older brother, Faizan, who was caught in a barn with a friend by some villagers. They called other villagers to the farm..."

"No," says Geri, their gut feeling a bit queasy.

"Yes," says Armaan. "They stoned Faizan and his friend. Killed them both."

Geri puts their hands over their head and sighs deeply.

"My dad told me about Faizan after Theo was punched in the nose. He said I was old enough to know what happened to his brother, the uncle I never met."

"Do you have other aunts and uncles?"

"Some in the old country and some who have come to this country. Dad says that most of them feel Faizan got what he deserved. He says he and mom will never be that way. It's why he volunteers each year to coordinate the bank's Pride event."

"Volunteers?" said Geri.

"You won't read it anywhere, but the bank's Pride event is dedicated to his brother, in my father's heart."

*   *   *

At work, Jorge gets into an argument with a Costco customer who feels the line at the cash is moving too slowly.

"Too slowly?" says Jorge. "Do you see how much crap the people in front of you have?"

"Hey," says a customer in the line. "You can't call my stuff crap."

Jorge picks up a bottle. "You don't call Focus Factor pills for brain acuity crap?" He points at another product. "You don't call a Kirkland Nativity Scene in June, crap?"

The customer who was complaining about the line moving too slowly shouts, "The line would move a lot faster if you'd shut your mouth and did your job."

"Well guess what?" Jorge says. "Your line just got a lot slower." He pulls off his Costco name tag, tosses it on the conveyer belt, and heads toward the exit. As he passes the customer service desk he calls to the Costco employees staffing it, "You can tell management that Jorge has left the building. Because I quit."

Later that night, over a dinner of grilled cheese sandwiches, he tells Krystal that he quit his Costco job. After dinner, he calls Ramon. Faking a sore throat, he calls off their date.

"During dinner, you sounded fine to me," says Krystal.

"I am fine physically, but mentally I just can't stand the thought of telling Ramon that I quit my job and am unemployed, yet again.

"You have no problem talking to me about being unemployed," says Krystal.

"Krystal, I love you but I'm not in love with you. There's a difference."

A couple of hours later, Jorge is watching TV when Krystal comes out of Geri's room, dressed for a night of clubbing.

"You club a lot," says Jorge. "Do you have a secret lover at one of the clubs?"

"I do," says Krystal. "Her name is *Dance*."

"That settles it. You are gay."

"How so?"

"You called *Dance* 'her'".

"You might be on to something. I'll have to talk about it with my shrink."

"Tell you what, I'll set you straight, no charge."

"I'm on Medicare with the shrink. No charge."

"Metaphorically speaking. So, who do you dance with?"

"Lots of lovely ladies. They know how to boogie."

"And after your transformation operation, who will you dance with?"

"Lots of lovely… my gosh, I am gay. Not that there is anything wrong with that."

"Like I said, no charge."

*   *   *

During dinner the next night, Krystal makes an announcement: "I will be on the cover of *Heels & Toes* magazine. At least my feet, my protest high heels, will be."

"How so?" asks Ellie.

"I thought you were through with modelling," says Geri.

"Me too," says Krystal. "But I was dancing at the Q club in the Village and a lovely lady, Beverly Wiseman, said she loved my heels. I told her that I bought them to wear to the Junita protest.

Geri

She told me that she was a freelance photographer shooting the cover of *Heels & Toes*. Beverly asked if I might be interested in posing my feet, clad in the heels, for the cover. I told her that I was born to pose. Maybe I'm not done with this modeling thing after all."

After dinner, the first-floor doorbell rings. Geri gets off the couch and goes to the door. Jorge, Krystal, and Ellie hear them say, "Really? Good to meet you. Come in. Come on in."

Geri enters the living room with somebody behind them. "Krystal, Ellie, meet Ramon." He pauses and looks at Jorge whose mouth is agape. "Ramon, I think you already know Jorge."

Ramon nods and smiles. Jorge gets up from his chair but doesn't move forward.

"I brought you some soup," he says holding out a bag with a jar of soup in it. "For your throat."

"Throat?" says Ellie.

"Yes, it was kind of raw the other day... Geri, do you mind if we go into your bedroom for a moment."

"Okay," says Geri. "But the bed is not made and there might be dirty clothes on the floor."

Jorge ushers Ramon into Geri's bedroom and shuts the door behind them. "Good to see you, but what brings you here?"

"On the phone yesterday, you sounded like you needed some TLC." Ramon holds the bag out. "You use a landline so I did a reverse look-up of your phone number online and found your address. Thought I'd surprise you."

Jorge clears his throat. "Surprise? I'll say."

"Are you okay with this?"

Jorge motions to the bed. "Have a seat. I have something to confess." He and Ramon pull up the bedspread and sit down. "I'm sorry I couldn't meet with you. I didn't want to tell you that I'm unemployed. Again. Accountant. Men's clothing clerk. Insurance agent trainee. Costco cash register clerk. The jobs are descending and I can't hold on to any of them."

"So, you don't need the soup?" Ramon asks.

Jorge laughs.

"What goes wrong with your work?"

"I don't know. I'm just not a people person. I don't take orders well. I don't like my bosses."

"Were you a decent accountant?"

"I was good. But I was a square peg in a round firm. I didn't fit in."

"May I make a suggestion?"

"Make away."

"Have you ever thought of starting your own bookkeeping and accounting business, specializing in smaller clients?"

"Not really, but..."

"Exactly. And a year from now, when I've finished school, you might even be ready for a partner who can fuss over figures for you."

"My own clients. No co-workers, at least for a year." Jorge laughs again. "You might be on to something."

"Listen," says Ramon, "if you have some time tomorrow I'd like you to come to High Park with me."

"High Park?"

"To the playground. To meet Henry."

Chapter Eight

Geri snorts cocaine in the bathroom with Gaston before they take to the Klub de Komedy stage. Once on stage, they fumble with their carpentry belt which has slipped below their hips, brush back their rainbow-streaked hair, place their hands to the sides of their deep-set eyes, and peer into the audience. They take a deep breath, cough several times, and begin.

"Hello," Geri says. "Bright up here? No? Ah, but you are not up here so you wouldn't know..." They take another deep breath, cough, and hesitate a moment before they begin again. "I have to tell you something..."

They hear Gaston hiss from the wings. "Or maybe not."

"Or maybe not," they say and hesitate as if looking for words in their brain, which is feeling rather scrambled.

"Preachers. I was going to talk about preachers. What's up with preachers? Up is where they think they are going. No? Gawd-- spelled g-a-w-d, just so you know--I wish there were ten seconds of consciousness after death, just long enough for preachers to go, 'Oh shit...' and realize they were going to do nothing but feed the worms for eternity."

Geri pauses, shakes their head back and forth to clear the cobwebs, and finds their next words. "Hey, I'm going to be performing my routine, or a version of it, at a big bank Pride event. What the freak are banks doing holding Pride events? When did we get all caught up in... commercial Pride or whatever. I mean, is our pride for sale to the highest bidder?"

Geri pulls their hammer out of their tool belt and tries to twirl it like a gun, but drops it. They stumble and mumble their way through a few more minutes of attempted humour, take an exaggerated bow to no applause, pick up their hammer, and exit stage right.

*   *   *

When Geri gets home that night, Ellie is on the couch typing away on her computer. Geri mumbles "Hello" and tries to sulk off to their bedroom.

"What?" says Ellie "No 'how are you?' No telling me how badly you bombed. Or how great you didn't do."

"Tired," says Geri opening their bedroom door and entering the bedroom. They try to close the door behind them but Ellie leaps off the couch and holds open the door.

"Do you want to make out?" asks Ellie. Geri tugs at the door which Ellie is still holding and just looks at her, their face in a frown. "Figured," said Ellie. "Spill it." She shoves the bedroom door completely open, enters the room, and sits on Geri's bed. "I want the truth, the whole truth, and yada-yada truth..."

Geri groans and sits beside her on their bed.

"You drink, but not a lot," says Ellie. "You were never this way after sex. You don't do... Drugs! You are stoned!" Geri puts their head in their hands. "Out of your tree stoned. Grass? No. You're too paranoid on grass and swore off it... Oh my, cocaine. You are stoned on cocaine."

Geri flops back on the bed. "I just wanted to try it to see..." Ellie punches their shoulder, hard. "Ouch!"

"I just wanted to punch you, to see..."

"I promise, never again."

"Or I find somebody else to live with, and not make out with."

*   *   *

The next day, after lunch, Jorge and Ramon are in High Park, at the entrance to the playground. They see a woman pushing a child on a swing. "There." Ramon points to her. "Maggie and Henry."

They approach the swing set. Ramon introduces Jorge to Maggie, who gives him a warm hug. Then Ramon plucks Henry from his swing and lifts him high in the air. "Wee-eee...wee-wee-wee all the way home." Henry giggles and laughs almost uncontrollably as Ramon swirls him around. And then he stops in front of Jorge. "Say hello to daddy's best-est friend. Say hello to Jorge."

Henry giggles some more and reaches out to tweak Jorge's nose.

*   *   *

Ellie is at work, organizing the box office. Jane sticks her head through the box office door. "Have a second?" she asks.

"Always for you," says Ellie.

Jane hands her the USB stick with the play on it. "I liked it. A lot. Liked the characters, their interaction, the mix of comedy and drama. I can see this on stage, here at the Rainbow. It needs a second pass to produce a bit more dramatic tension between the main characters, the former couple, but it's good. I laughed a lot and I even got a tad teary in places."

"Thank you. That means so much to me... I've been playing with the non-binary lead trying cocaine and their ex-partner finding out and bitch-slapping the crap out of them, in a loving way, of course."

"Nice one. You'd have to establish earlier that they don't do drugs so it comes as a surprise to her. Don't need a highfalutin moral reason but establish that it's something they chose not to do. Revise it when you have time and let me give it another read. The sooner the better. No pressure, but I'm still reading plays for the fall season as we speak."

Chapter Nine

Geri takes to the Klub de Komedy stage. They pull up their carpentry belt which has slipped below their hips, brush back their rainbow-streaked hair, place their hands to the sides of their deep-set eyes, and peer into the audience. They take a deep breath and begin.

"I am not coming on stage tonight. However, I have to come on stage to tell you that I am not coming up here. I am not coming on stage because Robert Sorbian, the straight white male cultural appropriation comedian--who does what he calls friendly gay jokes, people of color jokes, and women jokes--is your headliner tonight. I refuse to perform on any stage on which he will be performing.

"The good news? He is doing a one-night stand. He won't be here tomorrow so, like Schwarzenegger," Geri grits their teeth, pulls their hammer out of their tool belt, twirls it like a gun, slips it back into the belt, and speaks with an Austrian accent. "I'll be back..."

Geri takes an exaggerated bow to a smattering of applause and exits stage right.

After several other comedians perform short warm-up acts, the Klub de Komedy master of ceremonies takes the mike: "Ladies and gentlemen, and other genders out there, give it up for a man with multiple personalities, none of them split, performing for the first time at the Klub de Komedy, your headliner for tonight, Robert Sorbian."

Robert bounds on stage to a solid round of applause.

"Evening folks... Folks. That covers everybody. Folks. Men. Women. Non-binary. Other. One simple word and we move on, which I am doing." He performs a short moving-on cha-cha on the stage.

"I'm here for one reason tonight. To get paid. I'm also here to make you laugh, so I guess that's two reasons... Wait, if you don't laugh, I still get paid, so I'm really here for one reason.

Geri

"Before I begin, I want to address the non-gender elephant in the room. Not that I am calling them an elephant. She, they... It's so confusing to remember to use plural words for a singular person... They could do with putting on a few pounds... They, have every right to dislike me. And the feeling is mutual. But I'm here headlining and making money. They is or are not. I'm just saying." He cha-chas again.

"But enough about that. They have got my funny-positive show off to an unfunny-negative start. Cultural appropriation my derriere! As if their Austrian accent was authentic."

In an Austrian accent, Geri calls from the back of the room, "Hasta la vista, baby!"

"Whatever. Let's move on... Tonight I will be introducing you to my friends of colour, Amber, Blaine, and Ebony. My female friends, Emerald, Cinnamon, and Fawn (she's such a dear). And my gay friends, Francis, Garnet, and Devon..."

Geri turns to leave the club as Robert continues. They see several other people walking out. Not a lot of people, but a few are heading in the same direction as them.

Two women come up to them and shake their hand. "Nice set," one says. "Short and sweet and to the point."

Another man comes up to them and slaps them on the back. "I paid money just to see you. You were barely on stage, but I got my money's worth!"

"It was worth every penny I wasn't paid," Geri replies with a laugh. "Every last cent."

Chapter Ten

Geri takes to the Klub de Komedy stage. They pull up their carpentry belt which has slipped below their hips, brush back their rainbow-streaked hair, place their hands to the sides of their deep-set eyes, and peer into the audience. They take a deep breath and begin.

"Racists. What's worse than racists? Homophobic racists. And worse than those creeps? Violent homophobic racists. I'd say that stupid violent homophobic racists are even worse but correct me if I'm wrong, if you are a violent homophobic racist, you are stupid. Or at least ignorant. No?

"In other news, I'm going to see a psychologist. But who does one see a psychologist about? Can I talk to her about any of you? Don't think that would go over well. 'You should see this nut bar who was in my audience the other night. Laughed at every joke. How crazy is that?' Won't do. How about talking about me? Kooky, crazy, dysfunctional, and all 'round psychotic... Me!"

After fifteen more minutes, Geri takes an exaggerated bow to a solid round of applause that sounds like white noise to them and exits stage right.

Backstage they see Penelope, a comedian who went on a couple of sets before them.

"Sounds like it went well," says Penelope.

"Thanks," says Geri, "As I've explained to Gaston, I don't hear much of anything out there while in my comedy trance."

"Gaston?" says Penelope.

"Haven't seen him for several days, but yes, Gaston."

"You haven't heard?"

"Heard what?"

"Gaston is... dead."

"He's what?" Geri takes a step back.

"Dead. Of a heroin overdose."

"Dead?"

"Sorry to break it to you. I thought you knew. His body was shipped back to Montreal for burial, so there will be no funeral here."

"Nobody has said anything on stage."

"It's our job to make people laugh, not cry."

"But still..." says Geri. "Still..."

*   *   *

Geri gets home. Ellie is on the couch, typing. She looks up. "How was it?"

"Gaston is... dead," Geri says.

"Gaston? Dead?"

"He overdosed on heroin, several days ago, but I just found out tonight."

"Are you all right?"

"Other than seeing him backstage on occasion and sharing cocaine with him one night, I didn't know him all that well... Still... Still..."

*   *   *

Geri, Ellie, Krystal, with rainbow-coloured facemask around her chin, Jorge, and Ramon are all sitting on the railing of the front veranda, swinging their legs.

"This railing is just wide enough to be butt comfortable," says Krystal.

"But if you are at one end of the line, it's hard to hear someone at the other end. You have to shout to be heard," says Jorge from one end of the line.

"What's that?" shouts Geri from the other end.

As they are sitting there, swinging their legs, Armaan and Theo come running onto the porch and duck behind them.

"What's up?" asks Ellie, turning her head to look at the kids.

"You'll see in a moment," says Armaan.

"They're coming down the street, from the north," says Theo. "More jerks from that Catholic high school.

"It hasn't been as bad since you gave your talk," says Armaan. "But just wait."

Soon enough, a gang of five older kids comes running south on Ossington and stops in front of the house. "Hey Pakis," the gang leader shouts. Hiding behind your faggoty friends won't help you." His buddies laugh.

"Good grief, homophobic racists," says Krystal.

"You think assholes like that would at least get the race of the people they are insulting right," says Armaan under his breath.

"What do you expect from freakin' idiots," says Geri.

Krystal kicks off her heels and moves off the railing onto the porch.

"That's right faggot, run and hide," one of the homophobic racists shouts at her.

"Not running. Not hiding. Coming down there to kick your butts," says Krystal.

"Oh, we're shaking in our boots," one of the kids shouts.

Geri, Jorge, Ramon, and Ellie jump off the railing onto the patch of lawn in front of the porch. Krystal walks down the three porch steps and joins them on the lawn. "I guess I took the long way down," she says.

"Five against five," the homophobic racist leader says. "Seems like a fair fight.

Armaan and Theo run down the porch steps and join the five amigos on the lawn. "Against seven," shouts Armaan.

Krystal puts up her hands. "One thing before we begin," she says. "Has everybody had their pandemic virus shot?" Everybody raises their right or left arm and pumps up their fist.

Krystal rips off her rainbow-coloured facemask and puts up her fists. "Then we're good to go." She charges forward aiming right for the leader. Her friends, including Armaan and Theo, are right behind her.

The fight begins, with both sides punching, kicking, and scratching. There are even some attempts at biting.

84

After a couple of minutes of fisticuffs, two police cars, sirens blazing, pull up on the curb in front of the house. Four cops, including Constable Jason Phillips, leap out of the vehicles, wade into the melee, and start to separate the combatants.

"Break it up or we pull out the Tasers," shouts Jason, "and you'll all go down shaking and puking."

Once they have the groups separated the leader of the gang shouts, "They attacked us. We were walking by and they attacked."

"Right," says Krystal, "after you called our friends here Pakis and called us faggots."

"Okay, let me see if I have this right," says Jason, looking at Krystal, "You folks threw the first punch in reaction to their racist and homophobic slurs?"

Krystal nods.

"Would you agree with that assessment?" Jason asks the gang leader.

The gang leader nods with a smirk. "They got violent, not us."

"Then here's how it's going to play out," says Jason, as the other cops move to their cars to radio in some information. "If you," he says to the racists, "want to press charges, we'll take this group in."

"What?" says Geri, Ellie, Krystal, Jorge, and Ramon in unison.

Jason holds up his hands. "And if they want to counter-charge you for committing hate crimes, we take you in too," he says to the racists. "Just so you know, the jail sentence for hate crimes is five times longer than the sentence for assault."

The racists mutter amongst themselves.

"What do you want to do?" asks Jason. "No charges, everybody walks. Charges, we call in more cars and everybody gets taken down to the station for processing."

"If we say no charges and they say no charges, we can go?" says the leader of the gang.

"That's what I said."

"We're going," says the gang leader.

"Okay with you folks?" Jason says to Krystal who nods her head and waves away the gang with a sneer.

Geri

Once the gang is out of earshot, Krystal says, "How did you get here so fast?"

"I transferred to your division not that long ago. Someone down the street saw the gang chasing your friends here and called it in. I didn't expect to break up a rumble though."

"There are times…" says Geri.

"… that cops are not complete assholes?" Jason asks with a laugh as Geri grins and nods their head.

"Their sentence would have been five times longer?" Krystal asks Jason.

"They don't seem like the kind of folks who would Google it to find out," says Jason.

*   *   *

The next day, while out for coffee, Jorge tells Ramon that he has registered his accounting business name, BLB, which stands for Bottom Line Business, and a website domain name, BLB.com.

Ramon congratulates him and gets up and hugs him. "You will be terrific, I just feel it," he says.

*   *   *

That evening, Krystal, with cuts and scratches on her face, goes clubbing and meets Beverly who takes a long look at Krystal's face. "I'm so glad we're only shooting your feet tomorrow," she says.

"Got that right," Krystal replies.

*   *   *

At the theatre, Ellie gives Jane a revised version of her play. "Hope it keeps you engaged."

"I am so looking forward to reading it," says Jane. "It goes straight to the top of the to-read pile."

Chapter Eleven

Geri takes to the Klub de Komedy stage. They pull up their carpentry belt which has slipped below their hips, brush back their rainbow-streaked hair, place their hands to the sides of their deep-set eyes, and peer into the audience. They take a deep breath and begin.

"I've been trying to figure out if I'm non-binary or transgender. If the former, I think I can get my partner--my former lesbian lover--back. If the latter, I'm screwed. Or can screw, once I get a penis.

"I decided to see a shrink about it. Was hesitant to do so. I mean, never mind sorting out my gender issues, what if she cures me of my psychosis? It's my psychosis that motivates me to get up here and speak, week after week, month after month--and to not give up no matter how little you laugh. It's literally how I can keep on getting up here and not give a shit about whatever. After all, I'm just a carpenter pretending to be a comedian."

They clutch their tool belt and hoist it up again. Then they pull their hammer out of their tool belt, twirl it like a gun, and slip it back into the belt. "I'm not going to tell you what the shrink helped me decide about my gender issues. But I'm still up here, you're still barely laughing, I still don't give a shit, so we know what impact she had on my psychosis." They bow to applause.

"What I am going to tell you is that I have a paid Pride gig coming up in a couple of days, on Saturday. The day before the Pride Parade. While you are all out partying like the wild animals you are at Pride events, I will be at the no-doubt sedate Canada One Bank Pride gala. Gala. Not event or party. But gala. I'll be performing a toned-down version of my routine. Supposedly. If I want to get paid, that's what I'll be doing." Geri pulls out their hammer and twirls it again.

"How badly do I need the money? Badly. And yet here we are how many days away from the gig? And I'm still not sure who will take to the stage. Psycho Geri. Or Pay Me Geri." Laughter fills the room.

Geri does ten more minutes of comedy, to repeated laughter and applause.

Just before they take an exaggerated bow and exit stage right, they say, "Many of you knew a comedian who frequented this stage. Gaston." He pauses for a moment. "Gaston is dead. Died in a clichéd manner, the way many actors, singers, and comedians die. Heroin overdose. It hasn't been talked about up here because it's nothing to laugh at. But still, I just thought that those of you who laughed at his comedy, and he was a funny fellow, would want to know."

Geri bows. They exit to silence.

*　　*　　*

Jorge and Ramon are enjoying coffee and donuts. Jorge is talking about his plans to start marketing his business, which amounts to getting fifty business cards, because that's all he can afford, and handing them out at some small stores in the neighborhood. "I'll couple my accounting experience with my brief retail experience," he explains.

"What if I give you a phone number that will enable you to land your first gig?" Ramon says.

Jorge shakes his head. "Cold calling. Not really my thing."

"No, silly. One call to a friend of a friend who is looking for an accountant for some tax work. I told him all about you and he said to have you call him. It's a small job but it has the potential for repeat business. The exact kind of thing you are looking for."

"I can't do that," says Jorge.

"Of course you can. You pick up the phone, dial, and say, 'This is Jorge, Ramon's accounting friend.'"

"You don't get it," says Jorge. "This is my business. I have to make it happen. I can't have my boyfriend bring me clients left, right, and centre."

"It is your business," says Ramon, "and this is networking, something all business people do to expand their businesses."

"Not with their boyfriends," says Jorge.

"Okay, you are right," says Ramon. He pulls a piece of paper out of his shirt pocket. "I have the name and number of somebody who needs an accountant. Call this person. If you land the gig, my finder's fee is twenty-five percent of your first payment." He slaps the paper down on the table in front of Jorge.

Jorge picks it up. "Twenty-five percent? Isn't fifteen percent the standard finder's fee?"

"Would you like me to make it thirty percent?" Ramon asks with a laugh. "First, you don't want a referral from me, and now you think I'm charging too much for it?"

Jorge lifts his hands in mock surrender. "Okay, okay, I'll take it. And if it pays enough, I can afford to get a website built so I can put my website address on my next round of business cards."

"Afford to...? You can't build websites?" Jorge shakes his head. "You only need a simple one to begin with. I can do that." Jorge puts one hand up as if to stop Ramon. "Not for free," Ramon continues. "For twenty-five percent of your first payment from any clients you land online."

"Fifteen," says Jorge.

"Deal," says Ramon. He and Jorge shake hands. "At this rate, I may have to pay taxes this year."

"Not if you can find a good accountant. One who wants to earn his finder's fee back," Jorge says, grinning from ear to ear.

When Jorge gets home, he tells Geri, Ellie, and Krystal, "Ramon is building a website for me. We're putting the house phone number on it since I can't afford a mobile phone, at least not yet. So if the phone rings, effective tomorrow, you have to answer 'BLB.' If it's for me and I'm not here, take a message."

"And if it's not for you?" asks Gerri.

"You'll sort it out, I'm sure."

*   *   *

Krystal has buffed her heels so that they sparkle to such a degree it looks like she has diamonds on the soles of her shoes.

Geri

Beverly asks her to sit back in the chair she is on and to stretch out her legs. She tucks a soft, gold-trimmed pillow under Krystal's heels. "Cross your legs at the ankles," she says. Krystal does so. "That's good." Beverly moves Krystal's feet back a bit and fluffs the pillow around them. "Okay, let me adjust the lights and take a few shots," she says. "Then we'll try some other positions."

"My feet are posed and ready to go," says Krystal. "They'll go wherever you want them to go."

"Oh, and by the way," says Beverly as she adjusts her lights, "*Chatelaine* magazine has asked me to shoot their next cover. They are doing a post-Pride publication covering transgender issues, with a transgender fashion feature. If you don't mind, I'd like to put your name forward for the cover model. Your face should be nicely healed by then."

Krystal smiles wickedly. "From feet to face? You don't do photography for Girdle Magazine, do you? I feel like we should pause for some shots on our way up."

Beverly laughs. "Just put your best feet forward today and let's see where we go with things."

*　　*　　*

Geri meets Nadir at the door to the house just after noon. They are both on the way out.

"Too early to be heading out for a weekend comedy gig," says Nadir.

"But not a carpentry one," says Geri, lying about where they are headed.

"Did I tell you that Q-TV will be at the gala, taping a bit of your routine for their Pride feature? I presume you don't mind a bit of exposure on Q-News?

"Would be cool," says Geri. They pause for a second on the porch. "And I've been meaning to tell you that Armaan told me about your brother. I am very sorry about what happened."

"Thank you for that." Nadir sighs. "It's a screwed-up world. There is not much we can do about it, but we do what we can."

"Amen to that," says Geri.

Geri

"Oh, and I have to tell you something that I heard from Armaan," says Nadir. "According to the Internet, he is not gay, but he is gay-friendly."

"That he is."

"We like that about him."

"That we do." With that, Geri nods goodbye to Nadir and the two of them head off in opposite directions.

*   *   *

Geri visits Krystal's psychologist, Natalie Harmon, to discuss their gender state. They've been feeling more comfortable in the skin they are in for the last month, but the feeling vacillates and they still aren't sure if they are non-binary or transgender.

Natalie asks them a series of questions and nods appreciatively as Geri answers. She then says, "There are a couple of online quizzes I'd like you to take. They were developed by reputable psychologists and have proven to be exceptionally useful for people not sure about who they are in terms of their gender."

"An online quiz," says Geri. "To find out if you are transgender? Why didn't I think of that?"

Geri takes the quiz and then they and Natalie go over the results. After reviewing the results of the quiz, Geri takes another one. They review the results with Natalie again.

"Seems consistent," Gerri says.

"And how do you feel about that?" asks Natalie.

"I'm okay with it."

"We can talk more about it."

"I'm okay with it. I mean these quizzes nailed it, who I am and what I've been feeling, especially lately. But if you don't mind, there's something else I'd like to talk about with you."

Natalie holds out a hand, inviting Geri to proceed.

"You see, I have this comedy event coming up for a corporate crowd and I promised to tone down my routine, but I'm not sure that I can. I'm sure I can deliver a routine. I'm just not sure I can tone it down..."

Geri

When Ellie gets to the theatre that night Jane comes into the box office and slaps the USB key down on the ticket counter. "I freakin' love it."

Ellie laughs and applauds.

"September," says Jane. "It will be our first play this fall."

"Really?" says Ellie.

"You know what we pay?" asks Jane. Ellie shakes her head. "It's crap. A percentage, a small percentage at that, of the box office."

"I thought I'd have to pay you to put it on, so I'm ahead of where I could barely imagine that I'd be."

"Any idea of who should play whom?" asks Jane.

"You're asking me to help cast it?"

Jane nods. "We don't always have the author in the building when we put on plays."

"Elliot Page comes to mind for one role. And Kristen Stewart for the other."

"Right," Jane laughs, "and we'll get Jodi Foster to direct."

Ellie hugs Jane. "September? You could get Mickey and Minnie Mouse to play the leads, and Goofy to direct, and I'd still think that I'd died and gone to Heaven!"

"Don't know that Mickey would be quite appropriate for your play, but I get what you mean."

Chapter Twelve

Nadir takes to the Toronto Congress Centre auditorium main stage on Saturday evening, the night before Toronto's Pride Parade. "Good evening ladies and gentlemen and all other folks out there," he says. The auditorium is packed with almost 500 people. "Those of you who are here for the whole Canada One gala, I hope you enjoyed dinner," There is scattered applause throughout the auditorium. "Yes," says Nadir, "let's have a round of applause for those who prepared and served our delicious meal." There is more applause as Nadir clears his throat.

"The Congress Centre staff is working hard to clear the dinner tables in the dining space and will be opening the wall between our dining room and the room next to it. There will be lots of tables and chairs in the expanded space, a cash bar--everybody gets a free drink ticket--and a large dance floor so we can all dance to the smooth jazz sounds of Silver Spoon, our rainbow band for the evening." There is applause throughout the auditorium. "That, I believe, takes care of housekeeping matters." Nadir checks the notes in his hand.

"Now I would like to introduce to you our headline act for tonight. Straight from the Klub de Komedy, a non-binary stand-up comedian and an outstanding carpenter, ladies and gentlemen and all other folks, it is my pleasure to give you my friend and your comic, Geri Sender."

There is a solid round of applause as Geri steps in from the left wing and takes to the centre of the Congress Centre auditorium stage. They pull up their carpentry belt which has slipped below their hips, brush back their rainbow-streaked hair, place their hands to the sides of their deep-set eyes, and peer into the audience. They take a deep breath and begin.

"People who know me are surprised that I am here tonight. They say, 'You don't support commercial interests, especially when it comes to Pride.' I say, 'Don't support commercial interests? Wait until you see the opening of my Canada One act.

"A friend of mine, Jorge, is a freelance accountant. He hates networking because he feels he should do it all on his own. And he prefers to work for small companies, not large corporations. If you need an accountant, I want you to make his day. Go to BLB.com and email him. Tell him you need a freelance accountant and that you work for Canada One. And then tell him Geri sent you. Wham, bam, Jorge is going to go crazy." Geri chuckles thinking of how Jorge might react as laughter ripples through the audience.

"But if that isn't commercial enough, try this on. I notice that your advertisements and website feature a lot of individuals and couples. They are not all white, which is cool, but none of them look LGBTQ-plus. Get Krystal Orbit's phone number from Nadir and give it to your ad agency and website content developer. Krystal is a transgender model who should be your leading lady. Call her. Make it happen." There is muffled laughter.

"Ellie Bendy is a new playwright. I don't know the title of her play--she is keeping it secret from me--but it will be produced this September at Rainbow Theatre. She gets paid based on the box office take. Once her play is announced, go to the Rainbow Theatre website and book your tickets. Book 'em for entire departments and branches!" Applause ripples through the auditorium.

"And I'm a freelance carpenter." Geri pats their tool belt, pulls out their hammer, twirls it like a gun, and slips it back into the belt. "If you need any carpentry done, Nadir has my number." Geri takes a slight bow as more laughter greets their commercial opening. Nadir, in the wings, is shaking his head as if he is not sure how Geri's opening went over.

"And if I may segue awkwardly," Geri continues, "LGBTQ-plus rights in Canada are some of the most advanced in the world. But we still have issues. A friend was beaten up because she is transgender, although the miscreants who beat her called her a fagot, if I can use their language. Goes to show what they knew or didn't know. Another young friend was beaten up for being gay."

Nadir cringes in the wings thinking that Geri is going to talk about Armaan and Theo.

"I told him, 'At least in Canada you can marry the person of the same sex that you love.' 'So in Canada,' he said, 'I can marry the man of my dreams but be beaten up because I'm gay?'"

The crowd laughs in a kind of uncomfortable manner as Geri takes a deep breath.

"LGBTQ-plus relationships are illegal in seventy-four countries. In a dozen countries, being gay or bisexual is punishable by death. Forty countries have gay panic clauses that allow people to say, in defence of crimes such as assault or murder, that they were provoked by a gay, lesbian, or bisexual person." Geri pauses. "It's beyond crazy out there. It's deadly."

Nadir mutters under his breath, "This is too serious. Not at all funny."

"On a less commercial note, before I became a carpenter..." Geri again pulls their hammer out of their tool belt, twirls it like a gun, and slips it back into the belt. "...and an aspiring comedian, I was looking for full-time work. I have many flaws. One of them is that I cannot tell a lie. Let's face it, there are times a little lie is more suitable than the truth. 'No dear, those slacks don't make your butt look big.' Yes, even lesbians get asked that question by their partners." The audience laughs as if most of them have asked, or been asked, the same question.

"Anyway, I had several job interviews and the first thing I'd say is, 'I have to tell you that I am non-binary.' I was greeted by many blank looks from interviewers. 'Neither male nor female.' A lot of my interviews ended very quickly after my opening line. My point is, no matter who you are, you shouldn't have to hide who that is to land a job that you are qualified to do. Hell, over eleven percent of the Canadian population aged eighteen to thirty-four identify as LGBTQ-plus. With that in mind..." Geri pauses.

"Can I have the house lights up for a second?" Geri waits until the audience is bathed in light. "That means about ten percent or so of you are LGBTQ-plus. Can I have ten percent of the audience, the non-straights, raise their hands and, I don't know, maybe flap it about or twirl it around." They get nervous laughter, but no hands go up. Nadir is in the wings looking out at the stage. His brown face is turning crimson.

"Nobody? Point made. And this is Pride Month. We are at a Pride gala… Sponsored by a big bank. Could the sponsor, for whom you work, be why folks are too scared to be proud? Okay, you can turn down the house lights and we can all cower in the dark…"

Nadir is biting his hand. He wants to run onto the stage and haul Geri off. Instead, he flees the wings and leaves the auditorium muttering under his breath, "I am so screwed."

As the house lights slowly go down somebody in the audience shouts out, "I'm LGBTQ."

"Great, now that nobody can see you…" There is some nervous laughter.

"Turn the house lights back up and I'll say it again."

"House lights please," says Geri. They point to the middle of the audience where the shout came from. "Do you mind if I ask your name and, I dunno, the department you work for?"

"I'm Leslie, Leslie Durham in accounting. And I'm gay and tired of being hit on every day by the guys in accounting, some of whom I know are also gay but feel like they have to play the let's-hit-on-the-girls game if they want to get ahead."

From toward the back of the auditorium someone shouts, "Oh my gosh, Leslie, it's Sheena in Information Technology."

"Hi Sheena," Leslie shouts.

"Do you two know each other?" Geri asks.

"We're in the same dart league and play Mondays and Wednesdays at Crazy Joes, a pub down the street from head office." Leslie shouts towards Sheena, "I kind of thought you were…"

"And I wondered about you…"

"I sense a bulls-eye in the making," says Geri. "Are either of you here with anybody?" Both women say that they are not. "Tell you what," Geri continues, "everybody to the right of Leslie move down one seat. Sheena, you come on down and sit beside Leslie. Tonight, you are on a date."

People laugh good-naturedly as everybody moves down and Sheena comes racing down to Leslie's row.

Geri

"Didn't know I'd be matchmaking tonight," Geri says. "Anybody else want to confess?" They see a hand near the front of the audience go up. "We have a taker. Name and department?"

A woman stands up. "Karen. I don't work here. I'm here with my partner."

Geri puts their hands over their eyes to look more closely in Karen's direction. They see men sitting on either side of Karen, which confuses them because they think Karen is confessing to being gay. "Which one of those folks beside you is your partner, why does he look like a man, and does he want to stand up with you?"

"He's not beside me," Karen says. Then she shouts out, "But don't worry honey, I won't out you." Her voice quivers, almost in frustration. "I'm transgender and we don't come to bank events. But I really wanted to see you tonight..."

"Thank you for that."

"And so he got me a ticket, but the deal was we'd sit apart. I guess I embarrass him."

"Well that's kind of sad," says Geri.

"But it's not true," shouts a voice from across the auditorium. "She doesn't embarrass me. I'm so proud of her. It's just that..." The voice trails off.

"Name? Department?"

The man who was speaking clears his throat. "Samuel Mire. Finance. And I love Karen. I am just afraid of how people here would react and would treat me if they knew I loved somebody who was transgender."

"I think the cat is out of the bag now," Geri says, stating the obvious.

"And it's staying out, Karen. I promise."

"Okay, folks to the right of Karen, move down one seat. Samuel, come on down."

Samuel moves out of his row, runs across the auditorium to Karen, and embraces her.

"I have to ask, does anybody else want to confess to their LGBTQ-plusness? Going once, twice..."

97

A tall, greying man in a pinstriped three-piece suit sitting in the back row stands.

"Ah, I see we have another person who wants to confess. Name? Department?"

"Ripley C. Murdock, CEO."

"CEO? Sir, you're not? Are you?

"No, I'm not," Ripley says. "But my son is. I'm not outing him. He's at another Pride event with his friends."

"And?" asks Geri.

"He's going to change his last name. Says he doesn't want to be associated with a fuddy-duddy like me. And can I blame him? I accept him, but I have not been proud of him for being who he is. I have not been proud. He's a university graduate who works for a charity. Volunteers at a food bank. Visits his grandmother, my disabled mother, more often than I do. And I have not been proud of him... When he gets home tonight though, his fuddy-duddy father is going to give him one huge fuddy-duddy hug. And..." Ripley wipes tears from his eyes. "I'm not going to ask him to not change his name. If that is what he needs to do, so be it. But I am going to ask him to forgive me."

Applause fills the auditorium.

"Geri," Ripley continues with a chuckle, "I have to ask you, do you have tears at all your comedy shows?"

"Only my tears, sir. Only mine..."

Laughter and applause fills the auditorium and takes a minute to die down.

"And I'd say that's going, once, going twice, going three times..." Geri pulls their hammer from their tool belt and bangs the air in front of them three times before slipping it back into their belt. "Now the rest of my time up here is going to be really boring because it's time for me to be me, or for them to be them. I'm never sure about stuff like that. Miriam Webster hasn't yet produced the Non-Gender Dictionary. But before I have the house lights turned back down, may I ask again, how many of you belong to the LGBTQ-plus community?"

In response to the question, hands all over the auditorium start to go up. "Okay, I'm not good at math, but that looks like a solid ten percent to me." The proclamation is greeted with applause and cheers.

"Can we make it one hundred percent, for tonight?"

The audience roars its approval as everybody raises a hand.

You can turn the lights down now," shouts Geri.

With that, Geri rips into their act. "Patrick and Henry walk into a small-town bar. The bartender looks at them and makes a quick deduction. 'We don't serve queers here,' he says. 'We'll have two dry martinis then,' says Henry. 'I presume you serve them.'

A wave of laughter ripples over the audience.

"Speaking of walking into a bar..."

Geri does forty more minutes of comedy, to great laughter and frequent bursts of applause, most of which does not register with them in their comedy trance.

Nadir, who has left the building and is walking around the block, also hears none of it.

To a final round of applause, Geri shouts, "Thank you, folks. You've been wonderful!" They pull their hammer out of their tool belt, twirl it like a gun, and slip it back into the belt. They take an exaggerated bow and exit stage right.

*   *   *

Nadir is walking by the large glass front doors of the Toronto Congress Centre and sees people spilling out of the auditorium. He takes a deep breath to prepare to face the music and heads inside where he spots the bank CEO, Ripley C. Murdock. He thinks of dodging him but changes his mind and heads in Murdock's direction. Ripley sees Nadir walking towards him and motions him over.

"I'd like to say, sir, that I had no idea," says Nadir. "It was not the act we had discussed. Well, we really didn't discuss the particulars of their act, but it was not what I was expecting based on what I requested from him."

"I suspect not," says Ripley. "But then much of the first part was improvisation, so you never know what you are going to get. But what we got, my gosh. Talk about raw and honest. Even I got involved, which reminds me, I have to speak to my son tonight."

"Yes, gosh," says Nadir, having trouble reading Ripley.

"We don't know where Geri is. They seem to have left the building. A shy person, I take it, like so many performers. When you find them pass this message on to them," Ripley says.

"Whatever you have to say, sir. I will pass it on."

"The Q-TV producer said that they had their cameras rolling from your introduction and ended up filming the entire act. They loved it and wanted our permission to broadcast it. I told them we didn't have a broadcast agreement with Geri, but if they agreed to Q-TV's rate, it was fine with Canada One."

"Rate? Fine with?"

"We don't expect Geri to just give away their routine. Speaking of rates, didn't you tell me that you got Geri for half of what you were going to pay the comedian who fled to New York?"

"Yes, Geri was not as big a name."

"Do you still have money in the gala budget?"

"I didn't spend the savings on anything else."

"Then pay Geri the full rate."

"I take it sir that you enjoyed the show?"

"Enjoyed it? You saw me in tears there--of sadness and laughter. I don't think I've cried since I was five years old. And laugh? You'll have to excuse me now. I laughed so hard, I have to go pee. And by the way, I want to see you on Monday. We need somebody to review the bank's LGBTQ-plus hiring and on-the-job policies. I think you are the person to put together a diverse committee to do so. The folks who spoke up during Geri's routine might want to work with you on the committee."

"Yes sir. I will talk to Geri tonight and I will see you on Monday." Nadir then takes off to find the Q-TV producer so that he can watch Geri's entire routine and find out Q's broadcast rate before he speaks to Geri.

*   *   *

Geri

Geri is sitting on the couch, with their head in their hands, when Ellie gets home from work at the Rainbow Theatre. "How did it go?" she asks.

Geri looks up. "Let's see? I managed to call out a bunch of people. Embarrassed them into outing themselves in front of their peers. Got the CEO to out his son. All totally off script." Geri sighs. "Then I muddled through forty minutes of tedium, although I think I got some laughs. Oh, and I got overly commercial in ways that I don't want to discuss, but it might land Jorge some accounting gigs, Krystal a modeling job, and you a few more bums in seats for your play, whatever it is called…

Ellie laughs. "What? You? Commercial?"

"And Ellie, I totally reneged on my deal with Nadir. Did not pull a single punch. Not only is he not going to pay me, but he's going to evict us. Maybe even tonight."

Ellie sits down beside them and wraps her arms around Geri's shoulders. "I am so proud of who you are and so proud of you for being that person tonight."

"I can't be anybody else, no matter how hard I try. And I do try. I do. I just can't be non-Geri."

"And I will always love you for it."

Geri takes a deep breath and wipes their hands over their eyes. "While we're waiting for all hell to break loose, there is something I want to ask you. And something important I need to tell you…" But before Geri can say anything more there is a knock on the door to the apartment.

"It's too late for visitors. Do you think Jorge and Krystal forgot their keys?" asks Ellie as she gets up to see who is at the door.

Geri hears Ellie say, "We're still wide awake… No, you are not interrupting anything… Oh, why wait until tomorrow… Do come in." She comes back into the apartment with Nadir behind her.

Geri looks up, fear coating their face. Nadir looks down at them, shame coating his face.

"I'm so sorry," says Geri. "I didn't, I couldn't, tone it down. It's who I am. But I should have been honest with you and not taken the gig. You deserved better…"

Nadir puts up a hand to silence Geri. "May I have a seat?" he asks. Ellie pulls back a chair for him and he sits.

"I'll go hide in the bedroom while you two talk," she says.

Geri pats the couch. "I'd prefer it if you stayed here. Moral support." She sits back beside them. "Say what you have to say," Geri says to Nadir. "I promise I won't get defensive."

Nadir shakes his head and laughs a bit. "You are acting like you think I am here to evict you. And before I walked out on your show, that was my plan."

"Was?" says Geri. "Walked out?"

"You are right, you didn't pull any punches. You got so commercial off the top. Humorous, but oddly commercial. And then you got all political about the ugliness of it all, how the world treats the LGBTQ-plus community. And nobody was laughing and I thought my stomach was going to heave, and I left."

"So you didn't see it get worse?"

"I came back when it was over. You must have fled the scene."

"As soon as I was done."

"You didn't hear the audience react to you on stage?"

"I don't hear much of anything when I'm up there," confesses Geri. "I kind of go into my comedy trance and don't hear much. I mean if someone shouts out, as happened several times early on tonight..."

"You mean what Ripley described as the LGBTQ-plus confessions. When I saw the Q-TV video, it was incredible how you got people to come out. And then Ripley tears up while talking about his son."

"I am sorry about that. I didn't mean to make your CEO cry."

Ellie looks confused. "You two seem to be talking at cross purposes," she says. "Geri, you are saying the routine sucked the big lemon, and Nadir, I'm not sure what it is exactly that you are saying."

"Okay," says Nadir, "let me clarify everything. The show was a hit, a huge hit. The CEO loved that you made him cry and almost piss his pants with laughter. Q-TV wants to broadcast your entire routine. I saw their video. It's awesome. You know they are a cable

102

station and don't have a huge budget, but they are willing to pay you double what we paid you."

"That's..." Geri does some quick mental calculations. "...Six months' rent."

"And a larger hot water tank," adds Ellie.

"Wait," says Nadir, "let me clarify everything in the proper order, starting with a confession. I offered you half what I offered the comedian who went to New York, the person you replaced."

"Half of his rate is still way more than what I've ever made," says Geri.

"But," continues Nadir, "Ripley loved the show so much he's approved the original budget. We are doubling your rate, and that is the rate that Q-TV is paying you."

"That's..." Geri starts to count on their fingers.

"Eight months," shrieks Ellie. "And a new hot water tank!"

"And based on your show I have been asked by Ripley to spearhead a committee to review the bank's LGBTQ-plus policies."

"Sorry," says Geri. "I didn't mean to make work for you."

"Are you kidding? I'm in HR. People in HR live to spearhead committees. And because the bank CEO was so impressed with my work in finding you that he asked me to take on this review, I am giving you two more rent-free months in payment for what you have done for my career at the bank."

"Ten months," says Ellie.

"Listen," says Nadir, "I would like to apologize for trying to put comedy-content handcuffs on you. My brother... He would have been so proud of you for not listening to me.... I am so proud of you."

Nadir and Geri stand up. Geri holds out their hand. Nadir takes a step forward and embraces them.

The front door to the flat opens and Jorge and Krystal come spilling in.

"How went the show?" asks Krystal.

Nadir breaks his embrace and takes a step back. "I'm sure Geri will fill you in." He waves goodnight to all and heads for the door.

"Nadir," Geri shouts after him.

Nadir turns. "Yes?"

"Thank you so much."

"Trust me, it's mutual," he says and heads out.

"So?" says Krystal.

"Evidently it was a hit," says Geri.

"A palpable hit," says Ellie.

"And how was your evening?" asks Geri.

"It was a proud pre-parade party," says Jorge.

"Beverly and Ramon loved it," says Krystal.

"Beverly?" says Ellie.

"My foot photographer. We kind of started to date tonight."

"Kind of?" says Ellie.

"Yes, kind of," says Krystal.

"And Ramon and I have kind of started talking about moving in together," says Jorge.

"Kind of?" says Geri.

"Yes, kind of," says Jorge.

"Anyway, if you folks don't mind holding all the news for tomorrow, Ellie and I are kind of going into her room to talk about some stuff."

"Kind of?" says Ellie.

"Yes, kind of," says Geri, and they head for Ellie's room.

"Good," says Jorge, "because I kind of have to crash on the couch."

"And I on the floor," says Krystal.

*   *   *

Geri and Ellie are sitting on her bed, on top of the blankets.

"Nadir was happy with you, and for you," says Ellie.

"Only after he wasn't," says Geri.

"It's the final result that counts,"

"Which is what I want to talk to you about."

"Do tell."

"I had to confirm a feeling, a wonder, a doubt... I saw Krystal's psychologist. We had a really good talk. It helped me confirm what I was thinking but wasn't sure of..."

"Oh, spit it out," says Ellie.

Geri

"I'm non-binary, not transgender," says Geri. "I don't know if you'll take me back after all I put you through, but I had to work it out for myself."

"No penis?"

"No penis."

Ellie rolls towards Geri and plants a huge kiss on their lips. Geri kisses her back and then breaks the lip lock. "Wait a minute," they say. "I have a question for you too."

"Are you sure," says Ellie moving in for another kiss.

"Yes," says Geri. "Your play... What's the title of your freakin' play?"

"The title of my play?"

"Yes, for freak sake!"

Ellie laughs. "Gerrymander."

"Gerrymander?"

"Gerrymander... And crap, I have to rewrite the end of the darn thing!"

They both laugh. Then Geri says, read it to me, at least a bit of it."

"Seriously? It's so late."

"If you have time to make out, then you have time to read."

Ellie fishes for her computer on the nightstand beside her. She opens it. "Just the opening," she says. "In fact..." She clicks on an icon. "You read it. Out loud."

"Me?"

"Yes, you. I want to hear it in your voice."

Geri begins to read:

Living room, first floor flat. Terry and Elsie are sitting beside each other on a dilapidated couch. Elsie is eating popcorn.

Terry: It's less than two months until the Pride Parade. I know we're no longer together, but do you want to go to the Parade with me?

Elsie: I don't see why not. Unless you're with somebody else by then. Or I am. Not that I'm looking. In fact, if you were to tell me you've given up thoughts of getting a penis, I'd tell you that I've given up thoughts of breaking up with you. I mean I will always love you, but... Penis? A girl has got to draw the line somewhere.

Terry leans forward and reaches for some popcorn.

Elsie: Hey, you said you didn't want any.

Geri shuts the laptop and reaches over Ellie to place it back on her nightstand. They and Ellie embrace and kiss. But Geri breaks the embrace. "If you are going to let me spend the night here, we can tell Jorge and Krystal that they can use my bed."

"Tomorrow," says Ellie. "Tell them tomorrow."

Epilogue

Geri takes to the Klub de Komedy stage. They put their hands over their eyes and peer out into the audience in the small, dark room, take a deep breath, and begin.

"As you may know, Q-TV is here taping a special. Evidently, the Canada One Pride gala taping that they aired six months ago went over so well that the Q powers-that-be decided that they want another show. More of Geri getting paid to speak. Ya gotta love it. The only bit I haven't written, besides most of what I'm going to say, is the name of the show. Thought you could help me sort it out. I'll give you some names and you let me know what you like with your applause. Ready..." Geri clears their throat.

"Here's Geri..." There are a few laughs and a smattering of applause.

"Not that there's anything wrong with them..." Again, a few laughs and a bit of applause.

"The comedian is the message..." There is one hoot. "Ah, we have one, count 'em, one, Marshal McLuhan fan in the audience." That line gets laughs.

"A laugh a minute this isn't..." There are no laughs.

"I am not a funny them..." There is much laughter and a solid round of applause. "No, I mean that is what I am, or am not. A funny them. But hey, maybe you're on to something. Folks, we have a show name, I Am Not A Funny Them!"

Geri does another fifty minutes of comedy to great laughter, takes an exaggerated bow to hoots and applause, and exits stage right.

*   *   *

Geri, Ellie, Jorge, and Krystal are sitting in a bar in the gay village, sharing a jug of frothy draft beer. Jorge fills the glasses. Krystal pulls down her rainbow-coloured facemask to take a drink.

"The coronavirus pandemic is more than officially over," says Jorge.

"You can never be too careful," says Krystal. "The server didn't give us the vaccination salute."

"He wouldn't be working here without a vaccination," says Ellie.

"Still," says Krystal.

"Updates," Geri says. "Where are we now? Jorge, you first."

Jorge takes a sip of beer. "Things are going well in the freelance accounting world," he says. "Ramon is taking night school accounting courses and working as a partner in the business. He's in charge of the website and marketing and is starting to take on a few clients. We don't have Canada One as a client, but a number of our clients are Canada One customers, thank you. We're doing well enough to pay our rent, buy groceries, and dine out now and again. Ramon no longer has to bartend and he's upped his son's monthly support. In fact, we are planning a trip to France next spring."

Geri, Ellie, and Krystal cheer and toast Jorge.

"Oh, and I went to Rent-A-Wreck and paid them for the car we rented when we moved into your place."

"How much was it? I owe you half," says Krystal.

"With that magnanimous offer, how goes it with you, Krystal," says Geri.

Krystal chugs some beer. "As you know, my face was on the cover of *Chatelaine*. Beverly has been able to use me in several fashion spreads. Her business is taking off and I'm making a few bucks too. My face is on the Canada One website and in several of their ads. Photos by Beverly. Like Jorge and Ramon, we're doing well enough to pay our rent, buy groceries, and dine out now and again. In fact, we are taking a trip to the west coast, hiking in the Rockies, next spring…"

The friends toast and cheer Krystal.

"Ah, but I wasn't finished. The hike next spring is a month before my operation. I have a date for the surgery!" She raises her glass of draft in celebration and Jorge, Geri, and Ellie toast her and cheer again. "Pretty soon," says Krystal, "this lady is going to be, well, a lady!"

"This calls for more beer," says Geri.

"But before that, me," says Ellie.

"This I know," says Geri. "It's so cool."

"My play all but sold out at Rainbow Theatre. Many nights, the theatre was filled by staff from Canada One--entire departments and branches showed up. And the play has been picked up by CanStage. They are talking about mounting the show this fall." She chugs some draft as her friends cheer and toast her. "And... you'll never believe this, but I have two proposals from freakin' Hollywood: HBO and a film studio are in a bidding war over film rights."

Her friends cheer, toast her, and cheer again.

"Our rent is still paid from Geri's gig at the bank's Pride gala so we have no problem getting groceries or dining out. But hey," Ellie turns to Geri, "how come we have no travel plans?"

Geri waves at the waiter and points at the empty pitcher on the table. The waiter nods, picks it up, and heads for the bar. "Wait for my turn," says Geri and he says nothing more until the waiter returns with a new pitcher of draft and fills their glasses.

Geri sips a bit of beer, smacks their lips, and starts in on their update. "Nobody from Canada One has called me about any carpentry work. I guess they figure I don't hammer at a straight angle. However, Q-TV got solid feedback on my Canada One gala routine. And, as Ellie knows, the network has just shot a second show with yours truly that will run in the fall."

The friends cheer.

"What I haven't told Ellie because I just heard today, the Q-TV show was seen by a comedy club owner in New York. We have a vacation coming up!

"What?" says Ellie.

"I've been offered a five-night paid gig at New York's C Club next month. Plus all expenses--flight, hotel, three meals a day--for two, are covered."

The friends toast them again and cheer.

"Five nights of theatre on Broadway," says Ellie.

'What about my act?"

"You'll be doing pretty much the same thing each night, so I'll come to the opening night, and then… four nights of theatre on Broadway!"

Geri laughs and continues. "I got another call a couple of weeks ago, but I didn't tell anybody because it was not confirmed, until today. Netflix wants to come to town and shoot a one-hour stand-up comedy special at the Klub de Komedy!"

"Really," says Jorge. "Of whom?"

"Ha-ha," laughs Geri sarcastically.

"No. Freakin'. Way," says Ellie.

"This calls for even more beer," says Krystal.

"Way more!" say Geri and Ellie.

"Way, way more!" Jorge sings, and they all laugh and hug.

"Way, way more! Way, way more!" they all sing together. "Way, way more!"

About the Author

Paul Lima has had bisexual, homosexual, and heterosexual relations, his longest relationships being heterosexual. As a child, he would even wear his mother's clothes on occasion. He is currently asexual.

He has a lesbian sister, a gay brother, and a non-binary child. He thinks one of his aunts is gay but has hidden her sexuality under clouds of religious beliefs. But could she ever play baseball in her youth.

Paul believes sexuality is a spectrum and doesn't care where he is, or where anybody is, on the spectrum. He does not understand why so many people act as if it matters. He thinks they must be bored stupid. *Stupid* being the operative word.

Paul has been a professional writer and author for forty years.

Books by Paul Lima:

- *Family Tree: A Novel Spanning 17 Centuries*
- *Chronic: A Sick Novel*
- *Geri: A Post-Pandemic LGBTQ+ Novel About Something*
- *How To Write A Non-Fiction Book in 60 Days*
- *Tell Your Story: How to Write Memoirs and Autobiographies*
- *The Accidental Writer: A Memoir*
- *How to Write Winning Resumes and Cover Letters and Ace Job Interviews*
- *Everything You Need To Know About Multiple Sclerosis*
- *Everything You Wanted to Know About Freelance Writing - Find, Price, Manage Corporate Writing Assignments & Develop Article Ideas and Sell Them to Newspapers and Magazines*
- *Six-Figure Freelancer: How to Find, Price and Manage Corporate Writing Assignments*

- *Business of Freelance Writing: How to Develop Article Ideas and Sell Them to Newspapers and Magazines, Conduct Interviews and Write Article Leads*
- *The Query Letter: How to Sell Article Ideas to Newspapers and Magazines*
- *Produce, Price and Promote Your Self-Published Fiction or Non-fiction Book and eBook*
- *Harness the Business Writing Process: E-mail, Letters, Proposals, Reports, Media Releases, Web Content*
- *Harness the Email Writing Process: How to Become a More Effective and Efficient Email Writer*
- *Fundamentals of Writing: How to Write Articles, Media Releases, Case Studies, Blog Posts and Social Media Content*
- *How to Write Web Copy and Social Media Content*
- *Say it Right: How to Write Speeches and Presentations*
- *Copywriting That Works: Bright ideas to Help You Inform, Persuade, Motivate and Sell!*
- *How to Write Sales Letters and Email: Write direct response marketing material*
- *Unblock Writer's Block: How to face it, deal with it and overcome it*
- *How to Write Media Releases to Promote Your Business, Organization or Event*
- *Are You Ready For Your Interview? How to Prepare for Media Interviews*
- *The Atheist Chronicles: Why the Beliefs of Theists of Every Stripe Are So Unbelievable*
- *Rebel in the Back Seat, Hockey Night On Ossington Avenue, and other short stories*

For more information: visit www.paullima.com or email paulmslima@gmail.com.